The Depth of Unspoken Words

a novel by

J. Elise

Cover layout/design by Jasmine Hendrickson

ISBN:

978-0-947480-70-7

978-0-947480-71-4

Printed in the United States of America

First Printing, 2017

This is a work of fiction. It is not meant to depict, portray or represent any particular persons. All characters, incidents and dialogues are the products of the author's imagination and are not to be construed as real. Any references or similarities to actual events, entities, real people, living or dead, or to real locales are intended to give the novel a sense of reality. Any similarities pertaining to names, characters, entities, place and incidents is entirely coincidental.

Acknowledgements

It is with tremendous pride and gratitude that I am able to give all credit for the amazing design of my first published novel to my very own sister, Jasmine. I cannot list you all, but I must start with my mother Karmeta and father Kevin, thank you for always being there.

To my cousin Jimika, who has been more of a big sister my whole life, your encouragement, support and sassiness has helped me through not only this process, but life in general. My cousin Kyra— just the sweetest soul, thank you for constantly bringing the rainbows and sunshine and for keeping me company on many of those late night writing sessions. To all of my family and friends who have encouraged and supported me throughout this endeavor, from start to finish, I am forever grateful for you. To my colorful and supportive coworkers at American Airlines in Bermuda, much appreciation and love for your encouraging words and support.

To the amazing author and Book Boss Gaynete Edwards, who has not only become an amazing mentor, but a friend as well, I cannot thank you enough for everything you have done. Your support, knowledge and steadfast encouragement played a huge role in helping me to see this novel to completion.

Dedication

This novel is dedicated to Jahquae. A determined, loving and inspirational young lady. She is a fighter and has been a true inspiration for those who know and love her.

Chapter 1

"You will never be anything because of what I've taken from you."

Slowly opening her eyes, Simone lay there allowing her pulse to slow and her breathing to ease as the familiar words echoed and then slowly faded into her subconscious as the remnants of her dream faded away.

"I've let it define me, drive me...for so long."

Sighing and running a weary hand across her face, Simone slowly pulled herself to a seated position grabbing her iPhone in the process. Scrolling through her agenda for the week, she pursed her lips in slight annoyance at her first meeting of the day; a tedious yet essential meeting with her new department Head of Marketing division at BC Inc. Her annoyance was not because of who she was meeting, more so due to her hectic schedule. Simone had yet to read over the file her assistant had given her. She preferred to know in advance, certain details about whomever she came into contact with. Because of the sensitive and private information Mr.., she paused trying to remember the person's name, "Daniels, yes that's it." This meeting was prudent in order to go over, more like dictate, because Simone's word was often final, how such things would be handled. Placing the phone back on her nightstand she dragged herself out of bed and headed into her bathroom to start getting ready for her day.

Now with her mind in full work mode, Simone Caines, happy to have something else to focus on, headed into her walk in closet to get ready. Flicking the switch, recessed lighting brilliantly illuminated what many would call 'every woman's waking dream'. Such would be a fitting statement if one were to describe the size of it alone. Plush white carpets, which led to solid wood wall units, caressed her feet as she entered. The units were stained black and positioned on three out of the four walls. To the right of the entryway, one out of the three walls held shelves that went from floor to ceiling, full of designer shoes, sorted by color and style. The second wall contained two full length racks, top and bottom, which held custom tailored suits, all in a variety of shades of the only four colors you would see Simone in: black, grey, blue and ivory. The third wall contained two double full-length mirrors, both doubling as cupboards containing various designer bags and the remainder of her clothing. In the center of this massive room, with drawers on all sides, a solid wood island with dark grey marble countertop anchored the room.

Thirty minutes later, Simone walked into the foyer of her spacious penthouse apartment and greeted Ms. Davis, her long-standing housekeeper.

"Well, don't you look ravishing this morning! Are we dressed to impress or dressed to intimidate? "Ms. Davis asked playfully.

With her head down scrolling through her emails, Simone simply grinned at her, for she always dressed to impress, but her most flawless suits were usually worn when important meetings or business deals were on the agenda. Ms. Davis had been with Simone long enough to know the difference. She was a woman who payed attention to details and rarely missed a beat; not many people knew, or were allowed to know Simone so well.

"Yes, I have an important meeting this morning." Simone stated as she placed her phone in her briefcase while walking towards the island in the kitchen.

Ms. Davis knew not to ask nor was she expecting any specifics about said meeting, she simply smiled at the young woman she had come to adore as she placed her breakfast in front of her and proceeded to tidy up.

"Thank you Gladys, has Charles arrived yet?"

"Yes ma'am, I'm ready and waiting." Charles stated as he walked into the foyer. He too had been a long-standing employee with Simone, a year shy of Ms. Davis' seniority to be exact.

Grabbing the lightly buttered multi grain bagel and Togo coffee mug, Simone said her goodbyes to Ms. Davis and followed Charles to the elevator.

Chapter 2

On the drive to her office downtown, Simone thought about the graduation ceremony that would be held next week. She had been invited to be a guest speaker this year; it was an unexpected yet predictable invite seeing as her company was the main sponsor for their marketing program. At the end of her speech Simone presented one of the students enrolled in said program with the opportunity to complete a yearlong internship at BC Inc. They would be working under her newly appointed department head and were due to start in two weeks. If they were successful and proved beneficial upon completion of the internship, both Simone and the Head of Marketing would decide if they would then be hired for a full-time position. This was the reason for the meeting with

Mr. Daniels this morning. Simone would be informing Mr. Daniels that he had successfully been short-listed as one out of the two final candidates, and if successful, that taking on the new intern would be one of his responsibilities.

Thinking back to her - dream, Simone frowned at the fact that they were returning. She had thought her sessions with Dr. Phillips were helping. So deep in thought, Simone hadn't even noticed they had arrived at her building. Charles opened her door just as she pulled out her phone to place a reminder in her calendar to schedule an additional appointment. She couldn't afford to lose focus at this critical time.
"It doesn't have to limit me.."
Simone reminded herself as she stepped out on to the sidewalk. Without looking up she thanked Charles and headed towards the revolving doors.

"Ms. Caines you forgot your folder!" Charles called after her. Still preoccupied with her thoughts, Simone had forgotten it on the seat. Turning abruptly she didn't see but surely felt the force of the man she bumped into. The encounter happened so quickly Simone was knocked off balance. Strong hands kept her from falling and further embarrassing herself.

"Please forgive me!" Simone uttered. She dared not look into the face of whomever she had almost knocked over.

Charles rushed over. "Are you okay?" Both men asked simultaneously. Choosing the safer more familiar route Simone glanced at Charles, offered a weak smile and muttered,

"I'm fine, thank you Charles. I will see you at 6pm." Her pride kicking in instantly, she grabbed the folder, thanked the man without looking at him and hurried inside. Using her master key card, Simone hurriedly summoned an elevator and rushed in. She had caught a glimpse of his reflection in the door as she rushed in; it was one that only flustered her further.

Outside on the sidewalk, startled more by her beauty than the encounter, Kenneth Daniels adjusted his suit, gathered his wits and headed towards the same doors determined to follow her. Charles stopped him with a hand to his forearm.

"Great reflexes man." He said with a smile as he extended his hand.

Kenneth returned the smile as he shook his hand,

"Thanks. Well, I have a meeting to attend, good to meet you...?"

"Charles."

"Kenneth."

The two men shook hands and parted ways. Charles smiled at the encounter for there weren't many who could offset Simone. Kenneth rushed into the building no longer able to concern himself with finding the mystery woman; he was now in danger of running late for his meeting.

Chapter 3

Having recovered her composure, Simone exited the elevator, walked through the reception area and headed toward her office doors.

"The boardroom is set up for your meeting Ms. Caines."

Denise stated as she stood waiting outside of her own office which was just off of Simone's. She held out her agenda for the day. Grabbing the agenda, Simone breezed past her and headed in to her office.

"Let me know when Mr. Daniels arrives. Also call Dr. Phillips' office and see if she has anything available for either this week or next week, then see what my schedule will allow."

Not pausing to address Denise personally, Simone continued into her office and closed the door.

"Yes ma'am." Denise said more to herself as she sat down behind her desk. She was hardly fazed by Simone's somewhat dismissive demeanor. She had been Simone's assistant for five years and knew it came with the territory; it wasn't personal. She admired Simone for countless reasons: her drive, commitment and success as a woman and one who was young at that no doubt, was impressive; Simone Daniels could certainly hold her own in the business world.

In order to keep up, one had to learn quickly, to anticipate and adapt to Simone's demands and expectations. There was little room for error and there were standards that were unyielding, yet effective. Denise was fine with this because even though she had little downtime during her day, she was one who preferred to keep busy and she could never say her work or days were dull and boring. She glanced down at her personal copy of Simone's agenda that she kept on her desk. She smiled at the sight of Kenneth Daniels name at the top of the list. That was one fine man, and successful in his own right. She had been the one who handled the preliminary interview so she knew his background. Conducting the initial interviews was often her responsibility as it mainly entailed assessing the person based off of the specifics Simone set and gathering the requested information. Denise headed out to the reception area to wait for his arrival. Just as she'd sat behind the reception desk to start going over her workload for the day, in walked Mr. Daniels.

Walking up to the desk Kenneth Daniels smiled at the young lady who had conducted his initial interview.

"Good to see you again Mrs. Smith, how have you been?"
"Quite well thank you. Right this way I'll show you in."

Having done a little research on his potential employer, he had learned that Simone Daniels was a young and ambitious entrepreneur, one who had a reputation for being cut throat at times. She was a ruthless and shrewd businesswoman, which surprised most when they found out her age. Generosity was not lacking as one of her many qualities however, as she funded a number of charities as well as the allowance of the intern. In reference to her personal life, the information was quite sparse. He had decided not to look for any pictures, this one aspect he wanted to be a surprise. He knew that they were close in age he couldn't remember how close, but he preferred to visualize a seasoned, not too attractive woman; for ego and self-preservation purposes of course.

Taking a seat he thanked Mrs. Smith and waited patiently. Two minutes later he heard the click clack of Simone's Jimmy Choo heels as they came in contact with the marble floors, as she headed in his direction. A true gentleman, he stood in preparation to greet her.

Outside the door Simone paused to catch her breath. An urgent call in reference to one of the new products they were developing now had her running behind for the meeting. Taking a deep steadying breath, she closed her eyes briefly.

When she opened them she was in full business mode as she walked through the door.

That however, flew out the window when she came face to face with...

"You!" They both exclaimed simultaneously.

Simone regained her composure just as quickly as she had after their first encounter and walked over with her hand outstretched.

"Simone Caines, do have a seat."

Kenneth Daniels on the other hand, was dumbfounded as he tried to figure out if this was simply luck or fate. Snapping out of his daze he shook her hand, his manners kicking in.

"It's a pleasure, Kenneth Daniels. Please ladies first."

Simone's mind began to whirl as she thought back to when Denise had debriefed her on the interview with Mr. Daniels. She had found it odd and quite irksome that at the mere mention of his name, Denise could not help the however slight yet noticeable smile that graced her face. Simone would never admit it to anyone; she was barely admitting it to herself how handsome he was. It had been a long, long time since someone stirred in her what her brief and now chance second encounter with Mr. Daniels was having on her. Not since...

"No! I will NOT go there!" startled by the instant flashback Simone's anger simmered below the surface.

"Get a grip Simone! Business first! You do not have time for this." This was getting ridiculous. As soon as she was done here, the first thing that needed to be handled was setting up an appointment.

"I apologize for my tardiness; I had an urgent matter to attend to."

"That's fine, I understand. I haven't been waiting long."

"Right, let's get down to business." Simone stated putting that to rest.

"I was very impressed with your background and resume. Out of the few that were selected for secondary interviews, some with more experience, you stood out for your overall attributes — determination, passion and recommendations. What confirmed my decision in selecting you, as one of the final candidates for this position was the fact that you had spent time oversees taking under privileged children under your wing. Taking time to impart on and share with them what you had learned and experienced while obtaining your degree was what set you apart and impressed me most; something that is a rare occurrence."

Kenneth chuckled slightly, appreciating her subtle compliment. He had learned enough about Simone Caines to know that this was true. He was surprised however at her somewhat playful yet sincere manner. In most circles majority only saw her business and business only side.

Simone smiled ever so slightly, surprising herself at the playful and relaxed manner she seemed to effortlessly adopt while talking with him. Few knew what drove her determination to not only succeed but to reach out to those who were underprivileged.

"Well Mr. Daniels," Simone began, "I would like to say congratulations, and you've gotten the job."

Breathing a sigh of relief, Kenneth responded.

"Thank you! Thank you very much; I'm very grateful for this opportunity."

"It's my pleasure," Simone stated matter of factly.

However, in that instant, the moment those words left her lips, something shifted in the room between the two of them.

This was not like her, at all. Simone had structured her world, both business and private, to be run with the utmost control. So what was it about this man, with whom she did not know much beyond his three-paged resume that seemed to constantly throw her off balance? Kenneth felt it instantly as well. From their encounter outside of her building, being instantly intrigued by her without knowing who she was or who she would be, he had been captivated. Having just been given this great opportunity, as well as the fact that she was now his boss, a ruthless one at that, he was torn and knew he would have to weigh his options and tread lightly.

Simone glanced at her phone as a reminder popped up for her next meeting. She had at least ten more minutes before her next client was due, but truthfully she needed space to regroup. Buzzing Denise, knowing all the essentials had been covered, she would leave the tour and final paperwork for Denise to go over with him.

There was one thing she wanted, no needed to discuss with him herself.

"Okay Mr. Daniels, I must apologize for my sudden departure but I do have another meeting to attend. I would like to discuss with you, hopefully later this afternoon if my schedule permits it, the preliminary preparations for the graduation ceremony next week. As head of that department you will be presenting the chosen intern with the reward once my speech is complete and I announce the chosen student."

Kenneth was somewhat caught off guard by her sudden switch back to 'all things business' demeanor; coming to the conclusion that this would be something he would need to get used to. Also, he had not been aware that she would not only be attending the graduation but giving a speech as well; he couldn't hide his surprise.

"I wasn't aware that you would be attending the graduation as well, let alone giving a speech."

"Yes, the university invited me to be their guest speaker and to give the commencement speech this year; this is mainly due in part to the funding we provide for their marketing division."

This woman continued to surprise him. There was definitely more to Simone Caines than she let on. He did decide however, that in that moment, he wanted to know more.

Chapter 4

Just then Denise walked in and Simone couldn't have been more grateful. Standing with her hand outstretched she walked over to Mr. Daniels.

"Mrs. Smith will handle everything else from here and once again congratulations. I must be going now." Kenneth returned her handshake and smiled.

Once their hands touched a jolt passed between them, causing Simone to withdraw her hand immediately.

Turning to Denise she took the folder she held out for her.

"Set up a meeting with Mr. Daniels for this afternoon if affordable, if not Monday to discuss the graduation. Get him up to speed and make introductions." she stated simply as she continued to the door.

Without so much as a backwards glance, just like that she was gone.

With eyes still fixed on the door through which she had departed, Kenneth was unaware that he had been caught staring. Denise cleared her throat, causing him to come out of his daze.

"My uh, apologies Mrs. Smith." Kenneth stuttered only mildly embarrassed.

Denise smiled slightly, not surprised in the least at his fascination; he was hardly the first to be smitten.

"No worries Mr. Daniels, shall we?" She gestured towards the table for him to have a seat. She handed him several papers as she began.

"Okay so I just have a few papers for you to sign, as well as an outline to go over with you. It mainly states what your role here will be, what you will be entrusted with, etc. If you have any questions I will be glad to help. Once that's all done, I can show you to your office—"

"My office?" Kenneth asked cutting her off. "I assumed I would be getting my own little cubicle!" He stated incredulously.

Denise laughed,

"Not at all. All of Ms. Caines' department heads have their own office space. Those that you will be overseeing will have cubicles." Kenneth couldn't help but laugh himself.
"I apologize for interrupting and for my reaction. It's just that, this day has been full of surprises."
Smiling Denise continued,

"It's okay, I can understand that. But yes, as I was saying, once we're done here, we'll get you set up with HR to discuss your health plan, pension, etc. They will then assign you your parking space; give you the garage pass, access codes and key pass. Once all that is complete I can show you around and introduce you to everyone and then I can show you to your office." Denise recited the usual procedure as if it was second nature.

"Wow, sounds like a lot to get sorted, but I am definitely ready to get started!" Kenneth stated eagerly. Laughing slightly Denise continued,
"Yes, it is a lot to get through but I guarantee you the process is a breeze."
They were quiet for a moment while Kenneth began filling out and signing the necessary paperwork. Once that was completed Denise rose from her seat,

"Shall we?" she asked
"Lead the way." Kenneth gathered his briefcase and handed her the signed forms.

A half hour later, Kenneth Daniels walked out of the HR department, passes and all necessary information in hand. As was with everyone whom he had come into contact with under Simone Caines' charge, Linda Smith, Head of HR was very thorough and informative. He headed back to the reception area to where Denise was waiting while he had finished.

Looking up as he entered, Denise smiled warmly and asked, "So was I right, smooth process?" Kenneth chuckled, loving Denise's easygoing manner. Already he could understand how she had not only been chosen for this position, but more so how she had kept and maintained, quite well from what he could tell, for all these years. Many people tend to look down on those in an administrative position, never once taking the time to actually consider everything that they are responsible for. To add to that stress, she performed flawlessly working for someone like Simone. In the short time he had known her, from their initial interview until now; he could tell that she didn't seem to let things ruffle her feathers easily. She flowed through any task given efficiently and effectively; he could learn a thing or two from her.

"Yes, everything went very smoothly and I am very happy with everything so far. Everyone whom I've met here definitely knows his or her stuff! Linda was a trip though!"

Denise laughed while shaking her head simultaneously at Linda. She was an older woman, with years of experience who possessed a wealth of knowledge.

She always handled herself in a professional manner, getting straight to business and getting all necessary things out of the way. She did however have the craziest sense of humor and flirted shamelessly with a, in her words 'fine specimen of a man right there!'

Rising from behind the desk and walking around to where Kenneth stood waiting, she gestured towards an adjacent hallway to begin the tour. Laughing again slightly she said,

"Come on let me give you a tour and introduce you around. Your corner office."

She paused for affect. Kenneth's eyes widen in surprise.

"…Will be the last stop on our tour. " Denise continued with a smirk on her face as if she hadn't missed a beat.

It took Denise about forty minutes to show Kenneth the five floors that made up BC Inc. She made brief introductions to those they passed on the tour, seeing as proper introductions would be made on Monday. Simone Caines held mandatory staff meetings for each department head and select employees from that department, one day out of the week to be debriefed, deliver and receive updates and any other business. She also held a mandatory general staff meeting for every employee the first Monday of every month, which will be this coming Monday; all formal introductions will be made there.   Denise smiled to herself at how her boss operated. The way in which she ran her multi-million dollar corporation was immaculate. It was hardly a coincidence that Kenneth Daniels had been hired the Friday before her general meeting. This way even though he was a new hire, he would be receiving any new information, projections for the month and summaries of last month's progress, etc. along with everyone else. This would also allow him to meet all of the department heads, as well as finding out who they were and what they were responsible for. Monday was also the day that Simone held her weekly meeting with the marketing division. This was the department that Kenneth had been hired to oversee.

Her employees will get a chance to meet him, introduce themselves and then be given the outline and expectations set by both Simone and Kenneth; starting the Friday before gave him the weekend to prep. Simone Daniels often came off as short, dismissive and unyielding at times, but she was far from cruel. She possessed high standards and expectations and expected them to be fulfilled when requested; she left no room for error. She was definitely intimidating and straightforward when setting unbending guidelines. Which if crossed or not adhered to, that was that. She was not unreasonable however, she valued and cared for her employees but she did not let anyone take her for granted. She had long learned and adapted the concept that a happy employee ensured a flourishing and productive workplace. She held an annual family fun day for all of her staff as a thank you for their hard work.

As the tour came to an end and Denise headed towards Kenneth's new office, she shared this bit of insight with him. She did this both as a courtesy but also as a warning, for she had seen how he looked at Simone. She liked Kenneth, thought he was a nice guy. He reminded her a lot of her own husband. But in the five years that she had been working with Simone, she knew that no one was let in to her world. Simone Caines often left many men wanting; she didn't want him to get hurt. The main deterrent was that Simone never mixed business with pleasure. That did not stop them from trying. Would Kenneth Daniels be the exception?

Arriving at the door, Denise turned and grinned,

"Ready?" she asked playfully. Taking a deep breath, Kenneth nodded eagerly.

Turning the knob and pushing the door open, Kenneth whistled lightly in response. Walking through the door in amazement, Kenneth turned slowly taking in the spacious office with an even more spectacular view of the city. His office had been equipped with a large cherry oak wood desk and matching conference table as well as a built in bookshelf to the left of his desk. There were two large brown leather wing backed chairs facing his desk.
"This is amazing.' Kenneth finally said.
Denise smiled; he had a lot to learn about how Simone operated. Gosh, wait until he sees Simone's office, she thought to herself.

"Yes it is lovely, isn't it? You are free to decorate it however you want. There is an office and furniture supply store two blocks from here that we have an agreement with. All employees get a 40% discount on any purchases." she explained, as she took in his once again surprised expression. Secretly though, Denise had been thrilled herself when she found this out. Initially when she had started she didn't have her own office. She was split between the large reception desk and a cubicle, which was stationed between the front receptionist area and Simone's office. After her first successful year and as more task and responsibilities became assigned to her, she had been assigned a smaller, but equally spacious office just off of Simone's.

"I can see why she holds her employees to such high standards and can understand why she expects so much from them." Kenneth said.

"Yes, that is true. She takes some getting used to but she isn't that bad once you get used to her." Denise teased.

"I see." Kenneth stated simply. His mind was whirling with all this new information to process all at once.

Noticing his deep consonance Denise decided to take her leave.

"Well if there's nothing else I'll leave you to it. You know where to find me if you need anything. It's been a pleasure Mr. Daniels and I look forward to working with you." Denise stated walking over to where he stood with a hand outstretched.

Shaking her hand Kenneth replied,
"Likewise, and for the last time, it's Kenneth. You have a good day Mrs. Smith."
Denise smirked arching her eyebrow at the same time.
Kenneth laughed in response

"My bad…Denise."

He walked over to the large bay window, which overlooked the city and part of the harbor. As he slowly took it all in, Kenneth pulled out his cellphone to call his mother and give her the good news. While he waited for her to answer, he couldn't help but smile at her reaction. After the third ring, the center of his world and the person who he thanked most for where he now stood answered,

"Mom I got the job!" he gushed, pride emanating from every word.

"Oh, baby that's great! I knew you would, and I am so proud of you!" Jackie Daniels beamed with pride. They had been through so much, but she had always instilled in her children to never give up and always stay determined.
They talked for a few more minutes agreeing to meet for dinner before his mother was pulled into a meeting.

They hadn't always had it all, but Jackie Daniels had worked tirelessly to be where she was now; CEO of her own interior design firm. She would be retiring in a few months and was going to be busy tying up loose ends before she handed over the reins to her VP, Kenneth's older sister Kendra. His mother was his biggest inspiration to succeed and his main supporter. That was mainly why getting this job meant so much. He knew how hard she worked to ensure that they always had what they needed and had always encouraged Kenneth and Kendra. He never knew how much she had truly sacrificed to afford them the education and opportunities they had been blessed with.

He could have easily found a home within her company, like his older sister Kendra had. Kenneth however, had taken a strong liking to Marketing and Business. While growing up both Kenneth and Kendra had spent a lot of time at their mothers company, and most of the staff were like family. He had gravitated to marketing as he spent most of his time shadowing Herbert Jones, the head of the marketing for his mother's company. Besides, he was just fine leaving the 'swatches and paint samples to the women in his family'. He had joked with his mother and sister during a conversation they had during a celebratory dinner after he had graduated and Kendra had just been promoted. But one thing he never forgot was a conversation they had long ago; she had made them promise that all they had to do was focus on their educations,

"And....mommy would take care of the rest. We are a team right?"

"Yes!" Kendra and Kenneth had responded simultaneously. Kenneth smiled at the memory.

Chapter 5

Walking over to sit at his desk, he finally began to take it all in. There was a state of the art touch screen computer and wireless printer sitting atop his desk; he quickly turned it on. Pulling out his briefcase, he began pulling out all that he had been given by Denise in preparation for the meeting he had on Monday. He did not want to waste one minute of this great opportunity.

Simone sat at her desk, facing the floor to ceiling windows that overlooked the harbor. Lost in thought, the view was lost upon her as she twirled idly one of her monogrammed

Tiffany pens between her fingers. A knock at the door broke her out of the trance.

"Come in."

"I just got off the phone with Dr. Phillips receptionist. She can see you at either 1:00pm or 6:00pm. I checked your calendar and this afternoon may pose a problem if any of your meetings run late."

Simone glanced up at Denise from over her computer. Such thoroughness and thoughtfulness is why Simone valued and appreciated Denise more than most.

"Thank you Denise, 1:00pm is fine." she agreed not wanting to prolong this — problem, any longer than it had to be.

Denise simply smiled and walked back to her office.

Glancing at her watch, *11:15am,* Simone picked up her phone and called Charles. Remembering she had planned to stay at work all day, she had told him to pick her up at 6:00pm, her usual knock off time.

"Good morning Miss Caines."

"Charles, I've had to schedule a last minute appointment today for 1:00pm."

"Yes ma'am. I'll be downstairs waiting for 12:30pm."

"Thank you." she hung up.

Having worked solidly for a couple of hours, Kenneth's stomach had decided to remind him that it was indeed lunchtime. Feeling that he had left himself at a good place, before grabbing his cellphone and wallet, he quickly emailed himself the list he had compiled for the items he wanted to decorate his office with. Feeling a huge sense of accomplishment, he headed out the door and towards the main elevators.

Just as he walked into the lobby he stopped in his tracks, not expecting the vision before him. Simone Caines had her back to him while conversing with Denise. He hadn't had a chance to fully take her all in, as their previous encounters had been brief. But now, as he leisurely walked towards where they stood waiting for the elevators, he couldn't help but notice how her tailored suit fit her body effortlessly and to perfection. Following her long shapely legs up to her tapered skirt that outlined thick thighs and caressed a behind that made his mouth water. He kept back a few feet as to not eavesdrop on their conversation; neither lady had noticed his presence. The bell dinged signaling the elevator, and both women walked in continuing their conversation. As they turned to face the doors, both were startled when they finally noticed him.

Denise flashed a welcoming smile, while Simone uttered a simple good afternoon and turned her attention over to the cellphone in her hand. Denise on the other hand started up a casual conversation with him.

Simone was merely acting interested in the scores of emails she was perusing. When in actual fact, every part of her was aware of this man and his presence. Her senses absorbed his cologne, a subtle yet powerful scent that brought to her an immediate sense of comfort. It smelled heavenly and fit him perfectly. The silkiness of his voice sent a shiver down her spine, which settled unmistakably between the apexes of her thighs. Feeling a slow heat rising up her neck, Simone fought vehemently to get hold of the control her body seemed to lack when around him.

"What was it about this man?"

The elevator dinged and she inwardly sighed with relief. Being the true gentleman that he was, Kenneth stepped aside allowing both ladies to precede him out of the elevator. On the way out, Simone's arm brushed against his chest ever so lightly, sending an instant flashback to when in her haste, Simone had been pressed against it when he had stopped her from falling outside her building. This only further flustered her.

"I've got to get out of here!" Simone thought to herself.

"Denise have everything ready for this afternoon at 3pm." She stated before hurrying through the doors towards Charles and her car.

Kenneth didn't know how to take her sudden departure, causing him to wonder if the connection he had felt earlier had merely been a figment of his imagination. There was no mistaking however, the burning sensation that the simple touch of her arm against his chest had caused. Sighing slightly, inwardly he fought with his waring emotions, resigning himself to the fact that that's all it would be. Outwardly, he managed to answer whatever question Denise had asked him, smiled and continued their conversation as they headed out onto the busy street.

Chapter 6

After grabbing a couple of sandwiches and chips from the deli, Kenneth and Denise headed to the furniture store. Denise was a great help and offered up helpful suggestions. Kenneth had shown her the list he had compiled and with the help of one of the sales assistant, they found the items that he wanted with ease. The sales assistant advised him that all of the items could be delivered tomorrow if he wanted. Turning his attention back to Denise Kenneth asked,

"Would it be a problem getting into the building over the weekend to get them delivered, it would be great to be set up fully before Monday?"

"Not at all. The access card that HR gave you allows all Heads of departments access after-hours. When we get back to work just mention it to security so that they'll be expecting the delivery. Usually there isn't anyone here over the weekend, so you will probably have the office to yourself." Denise informed him.

"Okay great!" Addressing the sales person again, Kenneth completed his order and they set up a time. Pleased with how smoothly everything was going, he walked out of the store with a smile on his face. Outside of the store he turned to Denise,

"Is there anywhere close by where we could eat our lunch? It's such a great day today."

"There is a nice park just around the corner from here that I usually go to eat my lunch, but I have a few appointments and meetings that I have to set up and confirm before this afternoon so I have to head back," she said apologetically.

Kenneth smiled. "Oh okay. Hey no problem, it's my unofficial/official first day so there's plenty of time right?"

Denise smiled in return, "Oh definitely."

The rest of the short walk back to the office building was a companionable one. Upon entering the lobby Denise pointed out the security desk and waved goodbye as she headed to the elevators. Walking up to the desk Kenneth smiled at the gentleman sitting behind the counter,

"Good day sir how may I be of assistance?"

"Good afternoon, my name is Kenneth Daniels and I've just started with BC Inc., I'm having my office furniture delivered tomorrow and was told by Miss Caines' assistant to advise security so that you would be aware of it."

Nodding his head in acknowledgment the man replied,

"Yes, Mr. Daniels, that won't be a problem at all. Since it is the weekend someone isn't stationed out front here, but we are in the main office. So as long as you give us the time and name of the delivery company, someone..."

He paused looking down at a clipboard,

"Well looks like that someone will be me," he let out a hearty chuckle before continuing,

"I will come down five minutes before, to look out and will direct them to the back entrance so that they can use the service elevator."

"Okay that is perfect! I'll be here at around 8:30 and the delivery is set up for 9:00am. I can't remember the name of the company but I can get that for you. It's a company that Miss Caines usually uses."

"Ah ok, well that helps. That will be Office Coop; we've dealt with them on several occasions. They are aware of how everything works so it should be a smooth process. I'm Bernie by the way."

Bernie stood holding out his hand to shake Kenneth's. The two shook hands.

"Thank you for all your help Bernie, I guess I'll see you tomorrow."

Jotting down the time and name of the company, Bernie bid Kenneth farewell. Turning and heading to the elevators, Kenneth glanced at his watch as he waited.

"Good, I still have 20 minutes left to my lunch break." Belatedly he realized he hadn't had a chance to call his sister and fill her in on the good news. He knew he was in for a bit of reprimanding. Not having received the call right after he'd informed their mother, whom he guessed had already told her. Kenneth shook his head and smiled as he pulled out his cellphone and dialed. The phone barely rang twice before she answered,

"I'm waiting…" was Kendra's less than welcoming greeting, but Kenneth could hear the smile in her voice. He laughed in response.

"Hey sis, I know I know I'm sorry. Things have just been so hectic after I spoke with mom.

"Yeah, whatever you say little brother! Either way I am extremely proud of you and since I already know about the celebratory dinner from mom…" she stated, pausing for effect, "I guess I'll see you later. Love you! Gotta go. Bye!"

With that the call was ended. Kenneth couldn't help but smile at Kendra's antics; it had always been this way between them. They were closer than close and always had each other's backs. Just then the elevator dinged its arrival and he stepped in as he mumbled to himself,
"Love you too."
As he turned, he reached out to push the button for the 20th floor. Looking up he was taken aback as he came face to face with Simone. Clearing his throat he stepped over making space for her to enter.

"Good Afternoon Miss Caines."

"Hello Mr. Daniels."

The elevator headed up to the 20th floor. The air got thicker in an instant. Kenneth adjusted his tie. Simone smoothed her now clammy hands on the skirt of her ivory two-pieced suit. In an attempt to break some of the tension, just as he was about to inquire about her morning, her cell rang cutting him off.

"One second, she stated to the caller,
"You were saying Mr. Daniels?"
"Oh it was nothing. Have a good day." Just then the elevator opened and he stepped aside to let her out. Before stepping out she gave him an unreadable look, thanked him and headed to her office as she continued her call. He stared after her a long moment, wondering what it was about this woman. Realizing he had less time now to finish his lunch, he hurried to his office. Stepping through the door, the moment

forgotten as a surge of excitement and pride rose up within him as he walked in.

Turning her attention back to the caller, Simone both cursed and thanked her I.T. specialist Barb for her timing. She had heard what Kenneth had mumbled as he stepped into the elevator, oddly saddened that he was apparently seeing someone. However, what pissed her off further was how much she cared. Tuning back in to her call,

"What is it Barb?" Simone asked somewhat distracted.

"I have the information you requested Ms. Caines. Would now be a good time to drop it to you and discuss the specifics?" Barb asked

Simone thought for a moment as she sat at her desk and pulled up her planner. She took notice of the note about the possible meeting this afternoon with one Kenneth Daniels. She was not in the right state of mind to be alone with him, especially not after her session with Dr. Phillips. Not one to ever put personal before business, begrudgingly she admitted that it wasn't pertinent enough that it couldn't wait until Monday; what Barb needed to discuss was.

"That's fine Barb, see you in 30 minutes," she hung up.

Pressing the buzzer, she summoned Denise into her office.

"Inform Mr. Daniels that I won't be able to meet with him this afternoon. Barb is on her way to discuss the changes to our software security. I need it handled before I leave today so that everyone can be briefed on Monday."

"Would that be all?" Denise asked after jotting down a quick memo.

"Yes," Simone stated simply. As Denise turned to head out, Simone stopped her.

"One more thing Denise, I know I can be a pain but I appreciate it. Have a good weekend." With that said she turned her attention back to her computer, mushy moment over; Denise effectively dismissed.

Denise smiled and thanked her as she walked out. Simone Caines was a conundrum that was certain, but Denise wouldn't dream of working for anyone else.

Chapter 7

Settling in, Kenneth got down to business as he finished off his lunch. For the next few hours he planned to work diligently to have his introduction, presentation and guidelines completed enough that after he got his office situated tomorrow, he would only have to add finishing touches and proof read. He had just hit his stride when Denise knocked on his door that was pulled to, but not closed. Glancing up he smiled,

"Checking in on me already?" He joked as he finished off the last sentence he was typing.
Denise chuckled slightly,

"Not exactly. I had attempted to reach you on your office phone, forgetting it hasn't been set up yet; that will be sorted before you arrive for work on Monday. I came to let you know that Miss Caines won't be able to meet with you this afternoon to go over the preliminary preparations for the graduation ceremony. You will however, after the meetings on Monday, have an extended meeting with her."

Kenneth ignored the slight pang of disappointment he felt at the news, replacing it with the determination to kill his presentation on Monday even more.

"Okay, that's no problem, he stated matter of factly. "That gives me the rest of the afternoon to finish up everything, so that all I have to do tomorrow is get this place set."

"All right, well I'll let you get back to it. If I don't see you before the afternoon is out, enjoy your weekend and all the best on Monday!" with that she headed back out front.

After adding the final point to his conclusion Kenneth leaned back in his chair releasing a satisfied sigh. He had completed his presentation and outlines and felt proud of what he'd accomplished. All that would be left to do tomorrow was to read over and review. Packing up his belongings, he prepared to head out. He glanced at his watch; he hadn't realized it was after 5:30pm.

"Damn, I'm more behind than I thought." He was due to meet his mom and sister in an hour. It would take him at the most two hours to get home, shower, dress and then head back into the city, with traffic. He shrugged it off as he headed towards the elevators. It made more sense just to wait it out and stay in the area.

After the tedious but necessary meeting with Barb, everything was in order. Over the past several months, Simone had been testing out several different systems in preparation for the expansion into publishing, which she had planned to start rolling out next year. No one knew that Simone not only had a passion for writing and was quite skilled at it. This had motivated her to also obtain a Master's degree in English, along with her Master's in Business Management. She loved reading as a child, still did. It was her escape from — everything.

Letting out a sigh, Simone urged herself to focus.

Having narrowed it down to two programs, there had been a few flags that had been raised during Barb's final analysis. Knowing how Simone operated she would want to be updated before proceeding in order to avoid having to back track. They discussed her findings and Barb would email the final results later this evening.

Seeing that it was 5:55pm Simone packed up her belongings and headed downstairs to meet Charles. She was exhausted and eager to get home. Today had been draining in more ways than one, but she was pleased that so much had been accomplished.

Across town

Kenneth walked into the restaurant five minutes before they had agreed to meet. Waving off the hostess, he smiled as he spotted his mother and sister sitting at the table.

"So how is she?" Kendra asked in replace of hello as soon as Kenneth reached the table. The smirk on her face wasn't missed. Ignoring her question he walked around to hug first his mother and then Kendra.

"Must I sit in the hot seat so quickly? I mean this is a celebration for both of us isn't it?" He asked before taking his seat across from the two most important women in his life. He couldn't help but smile at them.

"Sis, you're lucky we love you so much because I have no idea how else we would put up with you. Looking at his mother he winked, "Right mom?"

"Fine I'll leave it alone for now, but don't think I didn't notice you changed the subject on purpose."

Jackie Daniels laughed at the playful banter between her two children. They had grown so much and yet this was one of the few things that probably would never change. She too was curious about her son's interaction with Simone Caines. For even though she was a name well known in the corporate world, her reputation painted a different picture from the young beauty she had seen in the picture Kendra had shown her. There would be time to probe her son, and knowing Kendra could get carried away, she assisted in moving the conversation along. The timing was perfect since the waiter had just brought the champagne that they had ordered. Raising her glass, she suddenly fought back tears as she eyed the lights of her life.

"I know I tell you two all the time how proud I am of you and all that you've accomplished, but sitting here in this moment, the joy I feel is indescribable. I love you both and cheers and congratulations abound for team Daniels!"

"Here, Here!" The three clinked their glasses together in solidarity and celebration. Kenneth didn't show the raw emotion he felt, while Kendra— deemed the emotional one, didn't stop the few tears that fell. Their appetizers had arrived and wanting to lighten the happy but somber mood, rubbing his hands together Kenneth eagerly stated, "Now, let's eat!"

There was a companionable silence as the three dug in. After about fifteen minutes, usually being the first to finish, pushing his plate away and easing back in his chair, Kenneth broke the silence,

"She definitely wasn't what I expected that's for sure." Both his mom and Kendra looked up at his statement.

"How so son?" Jackie was the first to speak as the two finished their seafood chowder and too sat back giving him their full attention.

"We all know her reputation and from what little information I could find out about my new employer, it was correct in deeming her as a force to be reckoned with. But I was prepared for someone less... *fine and as sexy as—*"

"Young and gorgeous?" Kendra chimed in, enjoying this far too much.

"Young yes," Kenneth continued pointedly ignoring the other half of his sister's comment, "and according to her assistant and what I could gather for myself, there is more to her than meets the eye, things few know about—personally I mean; she's very private. Kenneth's voice tapered off slightly as he thought back to his encounters with her. Shaking it off quickly, less his nosey sister and perceptive mother notice and try and pry him for details that would surely have him blushing.

"I can already tell that her business acumen is why she's accomplished so much; she is clearly very driven and excellent at acquiring anything she sets her mind to. Everything was planned out precise and immaculately. She has very high standards according to Denise—"
"Who is Denise?" Kendra asked
Her assistant. She was the one I told you about, the one who had conducted my initial interview. She also finalized the necessary paperwork and formalities and then showed me around. Anyway, according to Denise, Simone Caines holds all of her employees to high and somewhat unyielding standards, but she certainly takes very good care of them and equips them with the essentials to ensure that her standards are met. For instance, as her Head of Marketing I get my own parking space and corner office and—."
"Corner office, whoa little brother!" Kendra exclaimed. Kenneth laughed at her outburst as he continued, "which comes with the main components: Desk, chairs, small meeting table and a built in bookcase. All of her heads of departments are allowed to decorate with anything else from a furniture store just around the block with a 40% discount

on purchases. Smiling, he looked over at their expressions of surprise, particularly his mother who had stayed silent. Kenneth continued to share the rest of his day with his family as they enjoyed their entrees.

"That sounds wonderful son and a lot to take on for your first day and upcoming first week, but I know you will continue to make us proud and it sounds like you left yourself at a decent point before you knocked off." Jackie beamed with pride as she made reference to his upcoming presentation.

"And you say you're going in tomorrow on the weekend to finish off? Couldn't you do that from home?" she asked

"Yes I could, but my things are being delivered tomorrow and I want to have my office set up and ready to start fresh on Monday."

"Wow that was quick." Jackie stated, thoroughly impressed with what she was hearing about how Miss Caines ran her company. Both she and Kendra had been a bit taken aback at him starting such a task on his first day, a Friday at that, but when Kenneth had shared with them Denise's explanation of the monthly meeting and his singular meeting with his staff and Simone, they were even more impressed at how she functioned. Moving the conversation along, they discussed all that Kendra had to look forward to and everything she would be taking on and preparing for once their mother retired. It was a very exciting time for all of them.

Once they finished dinner, hugging and congratulating her children, Jackie made them promise to come over for breakfast on Sunday. Kenneth and Kendra agreed before they parted ways. She greeted her driver and settled into the backseat of her car as Kendra walked over to where her husband Thomas sat waiting. Once the two had left, Kenneth took a slow stroll back to BC Inc. to collect his car and head home.

Jackie Daniels didn't miss much and had seen her sons' reaction when he talked about Simone. But she knew her son, knew how determined he was to succeed. She wasn't worried about him keeping it professional when it came down to business, but she also knew how determined he was when it came to something or in this instance someone he wanted. Not one to outright encourage office liaisons, she wouldn't be against it, but she could tell he warred with the obvious attraction. Only time would tell how it all played out.

Chapter 8

Simone made her entrance into the main foyer at 9:00am. Dressed in fitted black jeans, an ivory shell top, which was accompanied with a white blazer with black trim. With her iPhone in hand, the click clack of her black Louboutin red bottoms against polished marble preceding her as she walked in. Both Charles and Gladys, who had been standing in the doorway of Charles' office conversing, looked up in surprise. It was not usual to see Simone awake, dressed and heading out for something that she hadn't informed Charles, at the least about.

Ms. Davis who was usually off on weekends spoke first,

"I'm sorry Simone; I didn't realize you were going out. I would've prepared something light to go." Finally glancing up from her iPhone, Simone realized that in her haste to get to her office she hadn't thought to inform Charles that he could have the day off. Mentally going through her agenda for the day, Charles did not recall Simone mentioning going anywhere. Always prepared Charles said goodbye to Gladys and walked towards Simone.

"My apologies Miss Caines."

"Oh goodness no need to apologize it's my fault, I forgot to call you. I received some emails that coincide with important reports that need to be finalized before my monthly meeting on Monday."

"Okay. So where to?"

"Oh it's okay Charles I'll drive myself. Don't worry about it Gladys, I'll grab something downtown."

With that she headed out of the foyer and to the elevator. Walking into the underground garage beneath her apartment building, Simone headed over to the five reserved spots she held. All five contained her car of choice: Audi. Two of the spots held the personal cars she had gotten for Gladys and Charles. There was also an Audi Q5 SUV and Audi S8 plus--both which she was often driven around in by Charles. Then there was her personal favorite, a white Audi S5. Walking up to the driver's side, she deactivated the alarm and climbed in. Starting her car, Simone relished the few times she not only got to drive her baby, but also the times she actually drove herself. Swiping her card against the access panel, she adjusted her shades as she waited for the security gate to rise. Pulling out into the street, she headed out for the 20-minute drive downtown. Kenneth had arrived at BC Inc. at 8:30am as planned. After checking in with Bernie, he was thrilled to find out that the delivery company had arrived a few minutes early and were ready to start taking the items upstairs. By 9:30am they were done and now all he had to do was organize things to his liking.

Simone walked into the reception area just after 9:30am and as expected it was empty. Walking into her office she sat her briefcase down on her desk and fired up her computer. Having browsed over the email from Barb last night during yet another sleepless night, she began her usual method of breaking it down piece-by-piece -- getting straight to work.

Having lifted, sorted and organized his office to suit his vision and having worked solidly for three hours, Kenneth stood in the doorway and let out a satisfied sigh. Now he really felt as if he had begun to find a home here. He realized simultaneously that he had long burned off the breakfast he'd eaten before coming in. Grabbing his coat, he headed out to grab some lunch from the deli around the corner. Arriving in the lobby, just as he went to exit through the main doors, he realized he'd left his phone and wallet on his desk.

He began checking his pockets, hoping that he had a few bills. No such luck.

"Oh well." Sighing as he pushed the button to summon the elevator he was grateful for the building being empty, the doors opened within seconds. Walking into his office, there his wallet and phone sat on the edge of his desk, waiting patiently while silently mocking him. Grabbing them both he headed back out front.

Glancing at her watch, taking note of the time, Simone saw that she had been working nonstop for the past couple hours. Belatedly she also realized she should've taken Gladys' up on her offer to make her something for lunch, now she would have to go and grab something. The closest and most familiar option was the deli around the corner. She grabbed her jacket and headed out.

"Click, clack. Click, clack."

As he stood waiting in the foyer for the elevator browsing through his phone, Kenneth raised his head slowly for he was surely hearing things. He had sworn he was alone, not having heard a peep once the deliverymen had left.

"Click, clack. Click, clack."

There it was again. The faint noise grew louder as it approached the reception area.

"Who could that be?" he thought to himself. Before he could ponder the noise any longer it stopped right when the elevator signaled its arrival. Shrugging it off, he entered the elevator. Turning around, his breath caught as he came face to face with…

As she walked down the hallway, Simone suddenly stopped dead in her tracks when she heard the ding of the elevator arriving.

"Who could that be?" She willed her now rapidly beating heart to slow, as she tried not to panic. She had sworn she was alone, which usually was the case if and when she came in on the weekend. Not hearing anyone, she cautiously rounded the corner to where the elevators were and came face to face with...

"Miss Caines?"

"Mr. Daniels?"

Chapter 9

Kenneth stepped aside so that she could enter the elevator. Once again he wondered if this was fate at work or purely a coincidence. He tried to bring order to the thoughts racing through his mind. The last time they were in the elevator alone, their time had been interrupted by the phone call she received.

So caught up in their surprise, both had forgotten to push the button for the lobby. His mind finally kicking back into gear, being the one closest to the panel Kenneth hit the button for the lobby. They both were quiet as the elevator began its decent. Attempting to make small talk he turned slightly to face her. Surprisingly Simone spoke first.

"This is an unexpected surprise."

A slow and easy smile graced his face, causing her heart to flutter.

"Yes, I was thinking the exact same thing."

She easily returned his smile. This man brought a calming to her that both unnerved and comforted her.
Realization dawned on him that he had yet to see her smile. He decided in that moment that he quite liked it. If he hadn't thought Simone was beautiful already, he realized two things: he instantly loved seeing her smile and from that moment on, his mind was made up that he wanted to be one of the reasons that she did; caution be damned.

They both became silent for the remainder of the ride lost in their thoughts.

Having reached the ground floor, the elevator opened, effectively breaking the spell that had been cast momentarily, or was it.

"After you."
"Thank you."
"Were you done for the day?"
"Actually I only stepped out to grab something to eat from the deli."
"Great minds...so did I.

"Even though we're both heading to the same place, is it okay if I accompany you?" Kenneth asked.

Simone gave him a look that caused him to laugh out loud.

"Hey I'm just making sure. Especially with the way I'm looking at the moment— compared to you. "

Far from slumming it, Kenneth wore black jeans, a fitted black t-shirt and all black high-top sneakers. Knowing that he would need to be comfortable, he had dressed casual. Even in 'casual attire' the man looked fine to Simone — just fine. She blushed slightly at his subtle compliment.

"Oh please, yes, its fine."

With that settled, they walked the two short blocks to the deli. True to form, Kenneth held the door open for Simone allowing her to walk in ahead of him. Unintentionally, he took advantage of the unguarded moment he had to give her the once over. As she strolled up to the counter, her hips swayed seductively. The expensive material caressing her behind the way he longed to. *Damn.* This woman could work a pair of jeans. So caught up in his fantasy, he wasn't even aware Simone had placed her order.

"Next!"

Snapping out of it, he was only slightly embarrassed as he pretended to peruse the menu. He dared not look her way, for he knew she had caught him. What surprised him was that she didn't seem to mind. At least, she appeared not to mind anyway. The slightest of smiles could be seen on her face as they stood to the side to wait for their food. Kenneth was enjoying seeing Simone in this light. There was a playful, carefree, less guarded and not so serious side to her. He couldn't help but feel comforted that she felt at ease in his presence. In the back of his mind however, he couldn't help but wonder if this was simply a fleeting moment, and come Monday— it would be as if it never happened.

As they grabbed their food and headed out, similar thoughts were running through Simone's mind. They made small talk on the way back and then settled into a comfortable silence. She did not miss the lingering looks, subtle flirtation and compliments; it was odd that they didn't bother her. Such attention from other men had been shut down instantly. Pondering this thought, she realized it had a lot to do with his approach and overall character. He wasn't forceful or disrespectful, he oozed confidence but wasn't arrogant. Belatedly she realized it could also be because of her session with Dr. Phillips yesterday and the escape he easily provided from that. Shaking it off, Simone didn't want to bring the negativity into what was turning out to be a good day.

Thankfully Kenneth spoke again, drawing her attention away from her wayward thoughts. Since they were coming up on the park Denise had mentioned to him yesterday he decide to take a chance,

"Since it's such a nice day out, did you want to sit in the park and eat?"

Simone thought for a moment.

"Hmm there wasn't anything prudent that I need to rush back to work to complete."

And truthfully, she feared that on her own her thoughts would consume her. She was grateful for the peace he brought her.

"Sure that sounds like a good idea."

Kenneth was thrilled. He wasn't ready to leave her company yet.

"Alright pretty lady, lead the way."

"You're something else."

As they entered the park Kenneth turned to her and asked, "Is there anywhere in particular you would like to sit?"

"I usually sit at one of the tables over there by the waterside, hopefully one is available."

"Oh so you come here often?"

"No, not really, not for a long time. Things have been…" Her voice trailed off.

"Come on Simone, get it together!"

Noticing the less than subtle change in her mood Kenneth quickly changed the subject."

"Hey I know it can't be easy dominating the corporate world. I mean, you could have left a little room at the top for the rest of us! Sheesh!" He joked hoping to lift her spirits.

His statement caused a smile to slowly appear on her face. He could tell that something was troubling her. He was tempted to ask her about it, but seeing as they were just getting to know each other he knew it would be too forward. Since preventing her from falling to the ground outside her building yesterday, there was this inexplicable need to protect her. The more time he spent with her, the more certain he became that he wanted to know more. He wouldn't push the issue though; he knew he needed to tread carefully. For now he was grateful that making her laugh was enough.

"Aw perfect there's one table left, ladies first."
"Thank you."

Chapter 10

Holding her stomach, Simone doubled over with laughter.
"Stop! I can't breathe!"
Walking back to the table after discarding of their trash, he sat back down and laughed along with her.
"You are so silly; I can't believe you were really that kind of child."
Glancing at her watch, Simone was surprised that they had been there for over an hour. The park had been busy, but the two of them had been in their own world, the conversation flowing with ease from one topic to the next.
"Wow I hadn't realized so much time had passed." She stood, brushing off the seat of her pants.

"Neither did I. I had a good time though," Kenneth stated with a smile as they headed back to work.

Simone paused for a second, still a little hesitant. But there was no denying she had enjoyed herself.

"Yes, surprisingly, so did I. Thank you."

"My pleasure." His words caused a shiver to run up her spine. Clearing her throat Simone quickly spoke,

"So, are you ready for Monday? It's going to be a busy day."

Kenneth had noticed the blush that had slowly crept up her neck; one that he'd imagined placing soft kisses on, before softly sampling her full, kissable lips. He hadn't been willing to let the moment pass so quickly. But her question had quickly reminded him that she was indeed his boss, one whom he had yet to impress.

"Yeah I am. I'm eager to get started. That's actually why I came in today. Since we didn't get to meet yesterday, it gave me extra time to finish my presentation. Today, after setting up my office, I was reading over everything."

"Oh I see. I had wondered why you were there; I wasn't expecting anyone to be there. Usually I would have the place all to myself."

Arriving back at work, Kenneth once again held the door open for her. Walking over to the elevators, Simone reached into her back pocket and pulled out her key card. Swiping it against the keypad, an elevator arrived and opened within seconds.

"Whoa. I know there is no one else here but man that was quick."

Simone chuckled slightly as they entered the elevator.
"I have the master key card, even on a busy day the result would be the same. It will bypass all other floors as well."

Kenneth let out a low whistle.

"Impressive."
The rest of the ride up was quiet. Once the doors opened, he let her precede him out of the elevator.

Turning towards her,

"Are you done for the day?"

"Yes. I just have to grab my things and then I'll be heading home. What about you?
"I'm all done as well. I could wait with you while you waited for your driver if you'd like."

Simone smiled, "That's nice of you but I drove myself today.

"I see, well if you don't mind, I'd prefer to take advantage of your perks and not have to wait for the elevator."

"Sure." she said with a chuckle.

Five minutes later they strolled into the underground parking garage.

"I hope you enjoy the rest of your weekend Miss Caines" Kenneth said, not really wanting to depart from her.

"You as well. And please, outside of work call me Simone."

Kenneth's smile widened.

"Okay I'll keep that in mind. Where's your car?"

Simone just smiled as she walked over to her car just off to the right of the elevator and opened the door.

"I guess being the boss has its perks, right off of the elevator? Not bad. Love the car by the way."

"And yours?"

With a mischievous grin on his face, he looked over towards the parking bays reserved for her Heads of Departments. Being that it was the weekend and no other car occupied the spaces besides his, there was no need for words. There sitting in "bay 12" was the exact same car. Simone's eyes widened in surprise,

"What were the odds?"

Kenneth laughed at her reaction.

"Enjoy the rest of your weekend, see you on Monday… Simone." he said as he climbed into his car.

Simone would swear that in that moment, that she had never heard her name spoken so simply and yet so…sensually.

"Who is this man?"

Starting her car, she slowly pulled out of the garage and headed home. Her mind was full and her heart constricted. She could not ignore the obvious connection between the two of them. Nevertheless, she had to, didn't she? Yes, she was his boss, but that was something even she knew could be overlooked. As she drove through the city, her mind wondered back to her session with Dr. Phillips,

Simone sat in her usual seat in silence for several minutes. This wasn't usually how their sessions started, but due to the urgency in which this last minute appointment was made, Dr. Phillips patiently waited. She had been surprised when her assistant had delivered the message requesting an additional meeting, seeing that they were due to meet on Tuesday. Whatever it was Simone had felt it couldn't wait. Releasing a sigh, Simone spoke,
"They're happening again...the...nightmares."

Dr. Phillips didn't let the concern she felt at this revelation show. Looking at Simone, one could not see the vulnerability that existed and you were unaware of the internal battle that left emotional scars. On the outside, she was as she appeared to everyone: in control, confident and with no worries in the world. You would not be wrong in your assessment of Simone. Dr. Phillips had discerned as much from her own perception and experience. If there was nothing else that being a psychologist had taught her, it was that it is often proved to be true that the people who have been hurt the most, those who have true horrors in their past, are usually the ones seen to have it all together and are extremely driven. Having been victims of someone else's wrongdoing, they are however, the same people who have a hard time letting go of the shame. They had been making such good progress. What had happened? What was the trigger?

"How many dreams were there? Was it the same dream?"

"I've had two dreams...so far. I've woken up either before they've really begun, or after the same thing has been said and I cannot remember anything before that."

"I cannot help but find the timing to be odd and quite random. Do you have any idea what has caused them to resurface?"

She hadn't been able to remember or pinpoint anything specific during her session. Even now, as she pulled into her apartment building, parked and headed into the elevator, Simone could not think of anything that may have been the cause. She had told Dr. Phillips that she couldn't shake the feeling that something troubling was amiss. That feeling still nagged her as she walked into the foyer of her penthouse. After the surprisingly great day she had, she didn't want to spend the rest of it dwelling on something so negative. With everything in order for Monday, she wanted, no needed to find something else to focus on and occupy her time. After changing her clothes she headed into her art studio. Simone immersed herself in what had always been her escape for the rest of the weekend.

Chapter 11

Arriving at work almost a half hour earlier than his scheduled time, Kenneth pulled into his parking space at eight o'clock. Approaching the elevator he couldn't help but smile at himself as he passed Simone's reserved spot. After the great weekend he had, he'd awakened feeling energized and eager to get this day started. Part of his eagerness he knew, was due to the fact that this was the first time he would be seeing her since their impromptu lunch. He was unsure how she would act and even more uncertain about how he should act. Stepping off of the elevator he shrugged it off. Pondering it anymore was pointless and truthfully, today he didn't need any distractions.

Walking into the reception area, he once again found the office faintly lit and quiet; He'd expected such since majority of the staff here were due in between eight-thirty and nine o'clock. Walking into his office, even though he had just been there less than twenty-four hours before, it was as if he were seeing it through new eyes. Resting his briefcase atop his desk, he headed to the break room to make some coffee before getting situated. There wasn't much that he had to do in forms of preparation. Having had to cross back through the reception area in order to get there, he noticed the lights were now on and at least one out of the two computers had been turned on. Rounding the corner he could already smell coffee brewing.

Walking into the staff kitchen, he smiled as he found Denise as the source of the freshly brewing coffee.

"Good Morning!"

Turning to face him, Denise returned his smile.

"Well well, look who is here bright and early. Trying to make an even greater first impression?" she teased. Very rarely did anyone beat her into the office; Simone being the exception on most occasions.

"You're very funny, but no. I guess I am a little excited with it being my first day and all though.

"That's good to hear. Today will be a rather busy day for you, but very informative. How are you feeling about presenting and meeting your team?"

"I'm confident everything will go well. I'm glad that I will be presenting last, it'll give me the opportunity to get a read on everyone and the company as a whole."

"Yes exactly. The general meeting usually lasts for about two hours once everyone has presented and given feedback. An outline drafted by Miss Caines is handed out in beginning so everyone can follow along. And once that meeting is over, we break for lunch and then your marketing meeting should begin about an hour after that. Give you a chance to stretch your legs. I know you'll do great!" She said with a wink and a smile.

"Thanks for the vote of confidence. The meeting begins at ten o'clock correct?"

"Yes."
"Okay great, I'll see you then." Kenneth turned to make his cup as Denise headed out.

At 9:45am, Kenneth gathered his things and headed out to make his way to the main boardroom two floors below. Reaching the reception area he was surprised to see Denise standing there as if waiting for him.

Gauging his surprised expression she said,

"I remember my first day vividly; it helps to walk in there with someone you know."

"Wow thank you." He said appreciatively.
"Not a problem, especially since I'll ditch you soon after. I sit off to the side at a computer, keeping the minutes." The two laughed.

Reaching the double doors of the boardroom, one of which had been propped open, Kenneth allowed Denise to precede him in. Entering behind her, his eyes widened in amazement. As he stood there in awe, only one word came to mind.
"Whoa"
The room was massive! He had been expecting your average run of the mill boardroom, one that was equipped with your usual conference table and accompanying office chairs. He had been mistaken. This room was similar to the mini amphitheater he used to sit in at college. The tall ceilings were filled with brilliantly lit recesed lighting, which softly illuminated the room. There were ten long rows of tables that stretched from one side of the room, to the other. Twenty black leather office chairs were situated in each row, that swiveled in and out from underneath them. At the back of the room sat a small booth that he assumed was some type of control room. It had been outfitted with a medium sized window that overlooked the huge room. At the front of the room was a small podium, behind it a large projection screen.

Several heads turned momentarily as they spotted the new face—some he recognized from Friday, others were new. Everyone had gradually begun taking his or her seats.

Fortunately the seat just off of where Denise took her place behind the computer was open.

Glancing at her watch, Simone grabbed her folder containing the reports she had been forwarded from her staff beforehand and headed downstairs. She had been busy right from the start of her day and hadn't had a chance to think about anything outside of work. As the elevator headed down, her mind strayed to this weekend's events. Kenneth surprisingly hadn't been far from her mind and she wondered how it would be to see him after Saturday. She had to appear detached and in control, she didn't however want to seem as if she was giving him the cold shoulder; hopefully he understood this.

Arriving at the conference room door, she adjusted her custom fitted black tailored suit before opening the door.

Turning around in his chair Kenneth faced Denise. "I guess you won't be getting rid of me that easily," he joked.

Before Denise could respond, in walked Simone. All conversation ceased as she walked the length of the room to take her seat at the front. She made eye contact with no one except Denise, whom she gave an imperceptible nod. With that Denise stood and as she handed Kenneth a stack of papers.

"Just take one and pass the rest down."

"Okay thanks." Turning to his left, he handed off the stack to a fairly good-looking young woman who smiled openly at him.

"Why thank you." She said with a wink. Subtlety was obviously not her strong suit.
Smiling slightly to be polite, Kenneth was hardly fazed or interested. He quickly turned back around, just barely catching the glare from Simone before a mask of impassiveness replaced it.

"Whoa! Was that what I think it was?" he thought to himself. It happened so quickly he couldn't be sure. Secretly he was thrilled at her apparent—jealousy maybe? Before he could ponder this anymore Simone spoke.

"Good Morning everyone. Last month was a very busy, yet very productive one and I'd like to thank you all once again for all of your hard work. There are several points that we have to discuss today. But first I would like to draw your attention to our new Head of Marketing, Mr. Kenneth Daniels." Nods of acknowledgment went around.
"As this is his first day with us, before each point is addressed by each person, I would like everyone to give a brief, introduction so that he may become familiar with who each of you are and what your responsibilities are here.

"First one on the agenda…"

The meeting lasted two hours with everyone making introductions and being updated and informed. Simone was thoroughly impressed with Mr. Daniels. Although his presentation was brief since he was basing it off information given not obtained first hand. He expertly presented the information and gave promising projections and guidelines, all of which would be implemented this month and several months ahead. She also noted how many of the women were equally impressed and if not mistaken, smitten with the offices newest eye candy. Surprisingly this bothered her more than she cared to admit or knew how to address. Thankful for its completion, calling Denise over she asked her to have everything set up for this afternoon. With that she rose from her seat and walked out.

If Kenneth wasn't so proud of himself for a job well done, he was even more so having glanced at Simone and noted that through her steely resolve she was clearly impressed. This further confirmed by Denise's subtle thumbs up as she also mouthed *well done,* before walking out. He headed back to his office to eat the lunch he'd packed before his meeting this afternoon.

Just as he entered his office the phone began to ring. Walking over to his desk, he picked it up on the third ring.
"Good Morning, Kenneth Daniels speaking."

"Good morning Mr. Daniels." the voice on the other end replied. Kenneth broke into a huge grin as he sat behind his desk, turning his chair to look out over the city.

"Momma actually let you beat her in calling me first?"

"We both know how competitive I am. I'm sure she doesn't have the energy to even bother these days." Kendra said with a laugh.

Kenneth laughed as well, "This is true."

"So how did it go little brother? The Daniels name still leaving a lasting impression."

"You know it. I still have one more meeting to go though."

"Oh right, the one she holds specifically for your division."

"Look at that, you actually do listen to me when I speak."

"You must've caught me on an off day," she replied sarcastically. "Okay well that's enough time spent bonding dear brother. Gotta go! Love you!"

"Love you too." Placing the phone back on the cradle he couldn't help but shake his head.

He decided that he would call his mother after the meeting this afternoon. He had reviewed his outline and strategies with her after breakfast yesterday and would update her with the feedback given from Simone.

Chapter 12

Simone ignored the way Denise watched her speculatively as they sat in her office finishing their lunch. She hadn't told her about Saturday but she knew Denise didn't miss much and had taken note of the buzz Kenneth had created in this morning's meeting—it was one of her best and sometimes annoying qualities.

"Since you're finished, isn't there something that you have to do instead of sitting there idly." Simone asked in an attempt to distract her.

Denise casually glanced at her watch before responding, "I still have fifteen minutes left to my lunch break, I'm good.

Besides, I'm not sure why you're acting as if you don't love my company." She said with a grin.

Well that didn't work.

Simone rolled her eyes at her comment, refusing to outwardly acknowledge that she was right.

She's trying to hinder me from asking about this morning. Denise was hardly deterred, not easily dissuaded by Simone's obvious attempt at dismissing her.

"So, she began. Simone stifled a sigh. "Mr. Daniels created quite the buzz this morning didn't he?" Simone casually stood to discard her now empty lunch container and then headed into the bathroom. Returning from washing her hands, she sat back behind her desk and turned her attention to her computer screen. Denise continued not missing a beat. "His observations and ideas for upcoming tasks were impressive; I think he will do very well here. Good move boss." She said with a smirk. Simone still said nothing although she had heard every word. Her thoughts were similar; then again, she was hardly surprised by Denise's observations. This was one of the many reasons they worked so well together and truthfully, why she was allowed to be so close with Simone. Their friendship was something Denise valued tremendously and also used to her advantage in situations such as this. She knew she was getting close to reaching Simone's limit, but she just couldn't help allowing this one last thing to slip out of her mouth,

"He also seemed to acquire several— admirers didn't he?" Simone slowly turned her head to face Denise, but said nothing. There was no need; Denise got the message. Laughing out loud, she stood and headed out,
"See you later…boss."

Turning her attention back to her computer, a wisp of a smile slowly graced Simone's face.

Twenty minutes later

Kenneth picked up his binder as he headed to his next meeting. Denise had called five minutes ago to advise that Miss Caines was ready for him, as well as to inform him that their meeting place had changed. It would take place in Simone's office instead. Since he had never been in or shown where her office was, she would meet him in the reception area to show him the way. As he headed out front his mind once again wondered back to the unexpectedly great afternoon they had had together on Saturday. He believed that there definitely was a connection between them, but having not seen her in that capacity since then left him feeling a little uncertain. Still lost in thought he hadn't realized he had arrived into the reception area until Denise's voice snapped him out of his daze.

"Good Afternoon Mr. Daniels. How was your lunch?"
"I managed to make out okay without my new lunch buddy."
They both laughed.

"Right this way," she gestured with her hand as she instructed him to follow her down the hall just off to the right. They chatted casually during the walk down the long corridor.

"...And my office is just over there." She pointed out as they arrived at the end of the hall.

"This is where we part," She joked as she gestured towards two large dark wood doors. "Just knock and then go right in, she's waiting for you. Good luck!"

"Thanks. See you later." Taking a deep breath, Kenneth knocked on the door before pushing it open. He stopped short upon entering. Just when he thought this woman couldn't surprise or exceed his expectations anymore. The size of her office alone was amazing, not to mention the view. To the left was a seating area outfitted with a black leather sofa, and two accompanying black leather wing backed chairs, along with a rounded glass top coffee table sitting atop a gray area rug. Hanging along the stark white colored walls were six beautiful paintings just behind the sitting area; he tried to recall the artist but was unable to. A built in floor to ceiling bookcase occupied the adjacent wall. To the right of that was a relatively large stained black conference table with eight leather chairs surrounding it. The star of the show was a large L-shaped black solid wood desk, framed elegantly by the floor to ceiling windows, allowing for a spectacular view of the city and bay below. So caught up in admiring her set up, he hadn't noticed that Simone nor any of the other employees were nowhere to be found. Granted the office was huge, but a first glance he saw nowhere that she could be hiding. Just then, a sound from behind him caused him to spin around. Seemingly out of nowhere, Simone appeared out of a door he hadn't seen. This was due to the fact that it was designed to blend in with the surrounding wall.

Simone who had heard him come in was amused as she watched his attempt at playing it cool.

"Good afternoon Mr. Daniels, I apologize if I startled you. I wasn't expecting you for a few more minutes.

Kenneth would've been more embarrassed if he hadn't been disarmed by her beautiful smile, once again.

"Good afternoon Miss Caines, I was just standing here admiring your office; it's amazing. *Just like you.* He responded, returning her smile.

"Please have a seat," She said gesturing towards one of the chairs in the sitting area. "It's just going to be the two of us this afternoon."

"Oh...okay." He responded a little confused, a lot thrilled that he would be alone with her.

"Due to the fact that this is your first day and you haven't even completed a full weeks' worth of work, I decided that conducting the meeting next week would be soon enough. Also, since we still have to discuss the proceedings for the graduation, there was no need for the other members of your team to be present as they will not be there."

She said as a way of explanation to his slightly puzzled expression.

"That makes sense."

"I also wanted to let you know that I was very impressed with your presentation this morning. It not only reconfirmed my decision to hire you, but it was the main reason as to why I decided this afternoons' meeting was not needed."

"Thank you very much, that means a lot."

"You're quite welcome. Okay, let's get down to business. The ceremony is due to start at ten o'clock next week Wednesday. The dean has requested that we be there at least a half hour before. We will be sitting off stage in the beginning during the preliminary introductions; we then take our seats on stage just before the awards ceremony. Since I was chosen to be their guest speaker, I will be giving my speech just before the awards are handed out and when it is time to award the recipient of the Marketing award, you will come up and present it to them once I call their name. At the end of the ceremony when the certificates are being handed out, you and I will be assisting with that as well."

"Sounds like a busy morning! I am honored to be able to take part. Thank you again for this opportunity."

They talked about the ceremony and the recipient for the next hour or so.

"Well Mr. Daniels, once again thank you for today. You did an excellent job." She said as she stood with her hand outstretched. Reaching out to shake her hand, Kenneth smiled.

"It was my pleasure." His smooth voice and the implications that those three simple words created caused a blush to creep up Simone's neck and a shiver to run down her spine. Cursing her body's reaction to this man, Simone slowly withdrew her hand.

"I do hope you have a good evening. I will be out of the office the rest of the week so I do hope everything goes well for you."

Kenneth was disappointed at this news, but instead of focusing on her absence, he would look forward to seeing her and spending time with her next week.

"Likewise Miss Caines. Have a good evening." With that he headed back to his office.

Chapter 13

Graduation Day

Kenneth pulled into the parking lot of the university at nine-twenty. He had decided to arrive ten minutes earlier to give himself time to find the hall just in case he became lost, and also to calm his nerves a bit. Dressed in a tailored navy blue suit, he had paired it with a crisp white shirt. He adjusted his burgundy colored Armani tie as he made purposeful strides across the quad, drawing the attention of several admiring females. All of which were missed by him as his eyes zeroed in on the one singular thought he'd seemed to have since first meeting her—Simone. She stood outside the entrance of the assembly hall browsing on her iPhone. *Is she waiting for me?*

A surge of excitement coursed through his body at the thought. He hadn't seen her all week due to her being out of the office. He had missed her and wondered if she had missed or let alone even thought about him while she was gone.

As he approached the entrance he was trying to think of a funny remark to greet her with when she suddenly looked up from her phone and looked right at him, a genuine smile slowly appearing on her face. *How did she know I was here?* He wondered in amazement for he was still a good thirty or so yards away. As he approached her, he finally took notice of her outfit of choice and couldn't help but chuckle slightly as he shook his head at the thought of it—she too had donned a navy blue suit, with matching navy blue Louboutin pumps. She had paired it with a white silk blouse.

"I'm beginning to think you've been spying on me now." Simone joked as she gave him the once over.
Kenneth laughed out loud, "Well you know the saying, 'Great minds think alike."
"This is true." Simone said in agreement as she gestured for him to follow her inside.
"Allow me." Kenneth opened the door for her, allowing her to precede him into the building.
Just as they'd entered the assembly hall an older woman approached them and smiled brightly as she held out her hand to Simone.
"Miss Caines! It's so great to see you again, we are so glad you were able to attend."

"It's great to see you as well Mrs. Edwards and it is my pleasure." Simone said as she returned her handshake.

Turning her attention towards Kenneth, Mrs. Edwards smile widened.

"This handsome young man must be Mr. Daniels." she let go of Simone's hand and held it out to shake his.

"It's a pleasure to meet you Mrs. Edwards." Kenneth said.

"The pleasure is certainly all mine."

"Mrs. Edwards is the Dean here at GU." Simone stated.

Simone just shook her head and smiled at the older lady whom she had built an excellent rapport with over the years. The obvious flirtations would have annoyed her coming from anyone else. But she had long since known that Mrs. Edwards was a very happily married woman and had been for twenty-five years.

"If you two would follow me this way we'll get you seated with the others, we'll be starting momentarily."

Taking their seats, Simone removed the slim folder which she'd had tucked underneath her arm on her lap. The speech she had prepared for today's ceremony was one that she hoped would be one of encouragement and purpose. She was passionate about her work and determined to succeed. She didn't feel the need to go over it, her passion for what she did would make it effortless to recite. Very few knew what it had taken for her to get to where she is now; a past no one could imagine, hidden behind a successful self-made businesswoman.

A round of applause brought Simone out of her musings, as Mrs. Edwards retook the stage.

"Now graduates, faculty, family and friends, as many of you may know, our guest speaker today is not only the main sponsor for our Marketing program here at GU, she is also a self-made, successful entrepreneur and businesswoman. It is my tremendous pleasure to invite to the stage our guest speaker of ceremonies, Miss Simone Caines!

Looking over at Kenneth before standing, Simone winked and smiled at him as she stood and headed to the stage. His heart fluttered.

"Good afternoon graduates, faculty, family and friends..." she began.

Kenneth sat over to the side with the Dean and other faculty members and important guests. He sat in amazement as he watched Simone give her speech with such poise and a passion he had not seen before. He glanced around and noticed that he was not alone. Others around him sat there in awe as well.

"If there is nothing else you can take from what I've said here today, I challenge you to let this one thing remain constant in your minds. Rather than limit oneself to another person's actions or restrictions, let their inability always drive you to be better in every aspect of the word. Learn from the lessons faced in life and do not let them dictate how you will live your life or lessen your potential. You are your toughest competition, for there is no one else like you. The uncertainty and vulnerability that I am sure the majority of, if not all of you are feeling is expected, but it does not have to limit you. Many of you still probably have no idea what you want to do, but do not let that discourage you." She paused and took a deep breath before continuing,

"I know what it is like to be vulnerable and my journey to success was far from easy. I however, chose not to see that as MY weakness. Instead, in that moment of feeling lost—and I do mean 'lost', you must choose to see it as an opportunity to BECOME strong, for in time it was revealed that when one focuses on what they see as weakness in an individual, it is merely a reflection of them as a far weaker person. People will always be intimidated by a concept that they cannot grasp. In closing, I want to leave you with these last few words, a poem that I have written:

"Your journey has been one full of constant change

Full of triumphs of sunshine but still constantly darkened by rain

Success isn't merely a goal for it too is a journey

While some embrace this task, its trials have faltered many

Our lives are full of tunnels many dark for some time

But at the end of every tunnel the light of promise shines

You have reached the end of this tunnel for that you MUST stand proud

Walk on that stage and rejoice that failure was never allowed."

"I wish all of you the very best in all of your endeavors. Congratulations and thank you."

A thunderous round of applause followed as the entire audience rose from their seats to give a standing ovation.

Mrs. Edwards walked back onto the stage, smiling brightly at Simone.

"You were wonderful my dear! An excellent job!"

"Thank you." Simone said as she headed back to her seat.
"You did a fantastic job Miss Caines." Kenneth said as he turned to face her.
She smiled genuinely at him as she said, "Thank you that means a lot. And I told you, Simone is fine."
Just then Mrs. Edwards spoke again,

"We'd like to invite Miss Caines back to the stage along with her Head of Marketing Division. Mr. Kenneth Daniels, as we announce the chosen recipient."

The rest of the ceremony went smoothly after the presenting of awards and certificates were handed out. As everyone started to filter out of the hall, Simone excused herself to run to the restroom.

Kenneth who was sitting in the end seat stood up allowing for Simone to step out into the aisle.

"Would you like for me to wait for you here or out front?"

"The bathroom is outside the hall to the left I believe, so you can wait for me there if you'd like. Would you mind holding my folder for me?"

"Okay, I'll be waiting. And no, not at all."

"Okay, I'll see you in a minute." Simone held his penetrating gaze before smiling shyly as she headed to the restroom. He watched her as she walked away, once again admiring her curvaceous body. He also noticed he wasn't alone in his observations as he saw a group of men watching her. Immediately a sense of jealousy came over him, but what could he do about it. He took a calming breath as he walked out to wait for her. While standing just outside the door, Kenneth's thoughts consumed him. Just then a young woman walked up to him. He hadn't noticed her until she spoke, bringing him out of his musings.

"Well hello there."

He really wasn't in the mood, but not wanting to be rude, he begrudgingly obliged her.

"Good Morning."

"You looked as if you needed a friend so I thought I would come over and say hello."

Kenneth offered her a weak smile but said nothing. He had grown bored of her already and was trying unsuccessfully to come up with a polite way to dismiss her.

"My name is Kelly, and you are?"

Just as he was about to respond to her Simone had walked up to them. Placing her hand on his forearm she spoke,

"Honey are you ready? Mrs. Edwards is looking for us."

Kenneth and the woman just stood there, both momentarily stunned. His mind kicking into gear, facing the woman whose name he'd forgotten as soon as Simone had touched him, he simply said,

"Nice meeting you.

With that he turned his attention back to Simone, smiling affectionately at her as he took her smaller hand in his, as they began walking down the hall.

"Lead the way pretty lady."

As they continued down the hall still holding hands, Kenneth couldn't believe what was happening. Simone had caught him off guard with her actions and yet he couldn't have been happier. He hadn't expected Simone to do what she did, and the fact that she was still holding his hand revealed so much. He took notice of the envious and admiring glances and stares they received as they walked and his heart warmed at the moment.

What in the world has come over you woman?! Simone didn't know what had come over her, or what made her do it. She simply reacted off of instinct. What she did know was that when she had walked out of the restroom and saw that woman standing there talking to him, all rational thought went out the window. She had seen the way she was looking at Kenneth and she didn't like it-- at all. What had both thrilled and surprised her at the same time was how automatic his reaction was; as if it was the most natural thing for him, for them both to be doing. Even now as they continued holding hands, it was the best feeling she had had in a long time.

Breaking her out of her daydream, Kenneth finally spoke, "So where are we headed?"

"Well Mrs. Edwards wants us to take pictures with and without the recipient and I believe they take them in the quad just around the corner here.

"Okay, that sounds good." Approaching a set of double doors, begrudgingly Kenneth withdrew his hand from her grasp as he opened the door for her. Simone missed his touch immediately. Just as well, for as soon as they exited through the walkway, Mrs. Edwards and Kenneth's/Simone's new intern, Joshua Swan stood waiting with the photographer.

Chapter 14

"Okay, that should do it. I'll have them uploaded and sent over to the editor of the school paper. Glenn should have them up on the college's website in no time Dean Edwards." The photographer stated after he had taken the last photo.

"Okay Roger." Mrs. Edwards thanked the senior film major student before turning her attention to Simone.

"Once again Miss Caines, thank you again for attending, your speech was wonderful. I'll be sure to forward those images over to your assistant once I've received them."

"It was my pleasure, thank you for the invitation. And yes, I'll let Mrs. Smith know to look out for them."

Mrs. Edwards smile widened as she faced Kenneth,

"Mr. Daniels, it was a pleasure meeting you."

"Likewise." Kenneth returned her smile.

"Joshua congratulations again dear. If you'll follow me we can head over to the reception for all of the awards recipients."

Before bidding Simone and Kenneth farewell, Joshua turned to face them.

Addressing Simone first, he nervously held out his hand to shake hers,

"Miss Caines, I uh, want to thank you again for this opportunity."

"Your quite welcome, Mr. Swan." Simone stated simply, noticing the blush that slowly crept across his cheeks.

Clearing his throat, he turned and shook Kenneth's hand.

"Mr. Daniels, I'm really looking forward to working with you."

"So am I Mr. Swan. See you next week and be ready to put those ideas you had to good use."

Joshua smiled, immediately taking a liking to Kenneth's easygoing manner.

With that, he and Mrs. Edwards headed towards the reception.

As she stood watching them walk off, Simone then turned and found Kenneth looking at her, a sly smile on his face.

"What's so funny?" she asked confused.

"Looks like you have yet another admirer." Kenneth stated matter-of-factly.

"Oh please, he'll get over it quickly," Simone replied as they headed towards the parking lot.

"And what do you mean another?" she peered at him out of the corner of her eye.

Rather than respond Kenneth simply shrugged, that sly smile still present on his face. Simone was left to wonder at the implications of his statement.

Is he talking about himself? She silently wondered and to her surprise, secretly hoped he was. Such thoughts caused her heart to flutter.

As they approached the parking lot Simone pulled out her iPhone realizing she had forgotten to message Charles.

"Shoot. I forgot to let Charles know when we were done."

She hadn't been sure what time they would be finished and had told him that she would let him know at least fifteen minutes before, to give him time to get there.

"Charles, yes I'm ready now. I forgot to let you know beforehand. Are you in the area?" She paused, glancing at her watch as she listened to his response.

"I see. No it's fine, it's my fault. Okay." With that she hung up. Now she would have to wait.

Kenneth couldn't help but overhear their conversation. Noticing her slightly furrowed brow he asked,

"Is everything okay?"

She sighed slightly before replying,

"Yes and no. I had forgotten to message Charles when the ceremony had ended. Rather than have him sit and wait here, I had told him he could go back home. It's going to take him at least thirty, maybe forty minutes to get here now, with traffic."

Hearing this Kenneth didn't hesitate to offer her a ride, he only hoped she would accept. Once again he wasn't ready to part ways from her.

"Well if it's okay with you, I would gladly give you a ride home if you'd like."

Simone's eyes widened in surprise at his offer.

"Really? You wouldn't mind?"

Kenneth smiled,

"Of course not."

"Are you sure? You don't have any plans? I don't want to put you out of your way and —"

Kenneth halted her rambling as he lightly touched her arm.

"Simone, it would be my pleasure. I don't have any plans and even if I did, I'm not about to leave you here stranded and alone.

Simone just stared. "Okay. Let me call Charles."

"Alright my car is right over there."

Simone started to follow him, "No wait here. I'll bring it over." He glanced down at her heels, which he guessed were at least four inches tall.

Simone chuckled at his expression,

"I can walk just fine in these thank you."

Kenneth laughed as well, "If you say so. Even still, stay and make your call, I'll be right back." With that, he walked off towards where he had parked.

Simone looked after him in amazement as she called Charles. It took considerable effort for Kenneth not to sprint over to his car; he was that excited. He couldn't believe how things were playing out. Reaching his car he fumbled with his keys before remembering the keyless entry.

Calm down man damn!

Taking a deep breath he opened the door and hopped in, quickly starting the engine.

Moments later he slowly pulled up to the curb. Before Simone reached the passenger side door, he climbed out, walking around to her.

"Let me get that for you."

This man..."Thank you." Closing the door behind her, Kenneth took another deep breath before walking around to the driver's side. Just the thought of being alone and in such close proximity with her, had his manhood twitching with adolescent excitement. *Get it together man! Or else it's going to be one long ride— Damn it!* He cursed silently as his thoughts caused a myriad of images to flash through his mind.

As she waited for him to walk back around, Simone desperately fought to calm her nerves. This man was slowly affecting her in ways that set her body ablaze and had her feeling out of sorts. If she was to get through this drive, she needed to get hold of herself.

Sliding into the soft leather seat, he turned to face her as he buckled his seat belt.

"Okay, so where to?" Buckling her seatbelt as well, Simone proceeded to give him her address. Pulling off from the curb and heading towards the exit, Kenneth pushed a button on the console and soon the soulful voice of Maxwell flowed through the car.

Simone gasped. Kenneth glanced over at her as he took in her reaction,

"You like this song?" he asked as Maxwell sang about *'This Woman's Worth'*.

"I love Maxwell. And yes this happens to be one of my favorite songs.*"

Again, Kenneth was left momentarily speechless as Simone once again managed to surprise him. Easing back into her seat Simone closed her eyes, allowing the smooth melody and the subtle yet unforgettable scent of the man beside her to consume her.

Five minutes into the ride, his stomach had decided, thankfully to quietly remind him that he hadn't eaten since breakfast. Kenneth glanced at his watch: *6:15pm. I wonder if she'll accept my invitation.* He took his eyes off the road momentarily as he looked over at Simone.

Turning down the music slightly drew her attention. She turned to face him expectantly.

"I uh, was just noticing the time and I just remembered I haven't eaten since this morning. Would you uh, like to, get something to eat, with uh, me?" *I'm stuttering, great! What are you sixteen man? Get a grip!*

Taking a look at her watch she took note of the time. Simone looked back at him and smiled, "Sure I'd like that, where did you have in mind."

Her automatic acceptance helped to put him at ease immediately as he came to a stop at a red light.

"There's this great seafood restaurant about ten minutes from here, it's one of my favorite places to eat."

"Okay that sounds perfect." That settled, Kenneth pressed down on the gas easing the car forward into what was turning out to be an unexpectedly great night so far.

They arrived at the restaurant in no time. Since it was a weeknight, there was plenty of parking along the street. Kenneth eased into a spot just a few feet from the entrance and shut off the engine. Unfastening her seatbelt Simone reached for the door handle. Placing his hand on her arm Kenneth stopped her. A shiver quickly spread over her body. "Let me get that for you." With that he exited the car, quickly walking around to her side and opening the door. Exiting the car Simone found herself mere inches from him. Taking even the slightest step would allow her to taste the sweetness of his breath that at this moment caressed her cheek. The attraction that neither of them had been able to deny cemented them both in place. Kenneth's eyes lowered, "Are you ready?" he asked his voice barely above a whisper. "Yes." Simone simply replied.
Finally taking a step back, they turned and headed into the restaurant. Both were aware simultaneously that neither had been talking about food.

Chapter 15

"Mr. Daniels! It is great to see you again." Kenneth smiled at the maître d' as they walked up to his station.

"Good evening Marco, likewise. This is Simone Caines. Simone, meet one of the finest maître d's in town." he introduced them, placing a hand at the small of her back. The subtle, unobtrusive and yet effective action made it difficult for Simone to concentrate let alone formulate a sentence. Somehow she had managed to, as Marco shook her outstretched hand.

"Will your usual guest be joining you?" Marco asked as he began gathering the menus.

"No not tonight." Kenneth replied missing Simone's somewhat bewildered expression. "Okay, right this way." With that, Marco led them to their table, a secluded booth away from majority of the other patrons, but one that gave them a good view of the small stage where the house band set up.

"Can I get you anything to drink? Marco asked as he handed them their menus.

"Water with lemon slices is fine for now, thank you."

"I'll have the same." Kenneth said. "Okay. The waiter will be over shortly to take your order. Before I depart, please allow me to inform you about our specials this evening."

After he'd informed them of the night's specials, the two were left alone to decide. Kenneth had already settled on the catch of the day and took advantage of the brief moment he had to observe Simone as she continued to peruse the menu. He already thought she was beautiful, however the soft glow from the candle burning at the center of their table, made her look even more radiant.

Closing his menu, he placed it off to the side as he spoke,

"Have any idea what you're in the mood for?" Kenneth's question was posed innocently enough. That did little to stop the images that immediately flashed through her mind. Simone had never felt this out of control, her thoughts always guarded with one singular focus; work. Feeling she was able to speak without sounding as breathless as she felt, closing her menu she took a sip of water, grateful for the relief it provided to her suddenly dry throat.

"I'm having a little trouble deciding, everything looks and smells so good here," she paused. "Then again, you already know that. Having frequented this establishment with your 'usual guest'." She teased with a raise of her eyebrow. This last statement caused Kenneth to chuckle slightly. He hadn't seen her expression when Marco had asked that question, but he could only assume what it implied. Less she thinks any less of him, he wanted to quickly clear things up.

"The 'usual' that Marco was referring to are my mother and sister. We all love seafood and this place has some of the best and freshest dishes in the city."

"I see." Simone replied. There wasn't much else she could say. She was elated that it hadn't been another female. As if he could read her mind, he confirmed this exact thing,

"You are actually the first and only other person whom I've brought here."

She couldn't hide her surprise nor ignore the special feeling that washed over her. "Really?"

"Yes really."

For a moment the two just stared at each other, both unaware that the passion each felt was reflected in their eyes. It was as if they were the only two in the room. Just then their water arrived, effectively breaking the spell that had been cast.

"Good evening. Have you had a chance to decide what it is you would like to order?"

Simone had gotten so caught up she still had no idea what she wanted. Just as she went to reopen her menu, placing his hand atop hers, Kenneth stopped her.

"Would it be okay if I chose for you? He asked. Simone closed her eyes briefly, his touch bringing back memories of when he had taken her hand earlier. As with before, it felt heavenly. She opened her eyes and looked at him,

"You can trust me." He reassured her, giving her hand a light squeeze.

Unable to speak she simply nodded. For even though he was only talking about food, in this moment, Simone believed wholeheartedly that she could, and for the first time in a long time, trust not only him, but to trust period.

"Do you drink?" Simone nodded, "Not usually during the week though, but a glass or two shall be fine."
"Okay great. There is a white wine that would go perfectly with our meal."
"Okay." Kenneth smiled at her before turning his attention back to their waiter and placed their order.

Chapter 16

"This is amazing!" Simone had just finished another spoonful of the seafood medley. "And you were right. This wine is a perfect complement."

Kenneth smiled and his heart swelled with joy as he watched her enjoy her food. He was mesmerized at the sight of her licking the remnants of the lemon and butter sauce off of her bottom lip. Something he found himself eager to do. Opening her eyes, Simone found him staring.

"Is there something on my lip? Did I miss something?" She asked, grabbing her napkin she dabbed at her mouth.

"No."

"Oh."

Kenneth took a sip of the wine as he attempted to focus on something other than those lips. They were quiet for a few minutes as they allowed the unguarded moment to linger and then settle around them. No words were needed; both were willing to simply feel, getting lost in the moment and each other. Kenneth had been grateful for all of the unplanned, yet wonderful and amazing times that he had been able to spend with her. But if he hadn't known before tonight, he was even more certain that he no longer wanted to leave things to chance. His mind was made up, but he didn't want to address that tonight. No he was a patient man and wanted to plan it out perfectly. He knew she was guarded and that gaining her trust was a priority first.

As she finished taking her last bite, pushing her plate aside, Simone quietly observed the man across from her. Everything about him had been unexpected, completely catching her off guard. And yet, she couldn't remember feeling this at ease. Her world functioned with the utmost control, everything planned out perfectly. She couldn't overlook the fact that with each of their unplanned encounters, everything felt right. She hadn't known that she would feel such a relief at how easily things became in his presence. She was happy. In the back of her mind however, that ever-present fear lingered.

Kenneth noticed her deep in thought and wanted to break the mood.
So, he started, effectively bringing her back to the present. "How did you like my choices? Was everything on point?" he flashed a shy smile.

Returning his smile Simone nodded, "Yes, everything was amazing. I thoroughly enjoyed…everything."

"I'm glad you did." They were quiet for a moment as the waiter cleared their plates and placed the bill on the table. Without looking at the total, Kenneth simply handed over his black card. He laughed at the look Simone gave him.

"You were amazing today," Kenneth began, "I was able to see you in a completely different light, one that you expertly keep hidden from everyone else I've noticed. That poem you recited, I was pleasantly surprised when you had mentioned that you had written it yourself. It was really good. You certainly are full of surprises." He watched as a blush spread across her face. A timid smile appeared on her face, before being replaced with a more unreadable expression. He was sure he wasn't wrong in his assessment of her; it pleased him that she didn't seem to mind it. He smiled slightly at how quickly she recovered from her moment of timidity. She wasn't about to make this that easy for him; still, it was progress.

Simone had noticed over these past few weeks how very perceptive he was. She wasn't however, used to anyone in her life being daring enough or comfortable enough to observe her in ways only he had. What surprised her was how she hadn't minded him doing so.

She hesitated for a moment before opening up; this was all new to her. Then again, Dr. Phillips had suggested that doing just that might help. Simone had been going to Dr. Phillips for years and she had never mentioned anyone who had affected Simone in this way. Decision made.

"You certainly do not miss much do you?" She teased

"No, not really. Growing up in a house outnumbered by women, and having to deal with Kendra's antics specifically," he chuckled slightly before continuing, "I had to learn quickly to stay on my toes."

Simone laughed a little as well, remembering the few stories he had told her during their impromptu lunch.

"And yes, I prefer keeping everyone, well mostly everyone at a certain distance. It allows me a certain level of control and consistency. Today, speaking to the graduates, I remember what it was like being in their shoes. I'm sure you do as well. None of them will ever know me personally, so I was comfortable with what was shared, knowing it wouldn't go beyond that." She explained.

"I can see where you're coming from. How you explained that makes sense. I'm sure the vulnerability bit would be hard for them to picture though. You have quite the reputation." He grinned at her.

Simone rolled her eyes, even as she found herself laughing at his playfulness.

"You don't seem too intimidated by it." She challenged.

"Not at all. I love a challenge," was his daring reply. His eyes boring into hers with such intensity, it quickly sent a chill down her spine.

Chapter 17

Simone took a deliberate sip of her wine in an attempt to break away from the spell he was beginning to cast on her. Kenneth wasn't so willing to let the mood go as he eyed her speculatively. He placed his hand atop hers, her eyes slowly raised to meet his.

"Okay." This was the only word that properly formulated in her mind, as his subtle touch both comforted and unnerved her. Easing her hand away slowly, she glanced at her watch, *9:20pm.* "Wow! Have we really been here that long?" Neither had kept track of the time, so caught up had they been in the good time they were having. Kenneth eased out of the booth, as he stood he held out his hand for her. In his mind he wanted to take advantage of this time with her, in which she allowed herself to be more open.

For he knew that sadly, once they returned to work, a certain degree of distance and decorum would have to be applied. Again, Simone easily accepted his hand. In silence the pair headed out of the restaurant. Stepping outside, the temperature had dropped considerably causing Simone to shiver. Noticing immediately, Kenneth quickly shrugged out of his jacket and placed it over her shoulders.

"Better?"

"Yes, thank you." She replied shyly. Taking her hand in his again, they continued on the short walk to the car.

The drive to her home was a quiet, yet companionable one. The smooth sounds of R&B filled the gaps between the unspoken words, further securing for them both this undeniable connection. As he turned onto her street, approaching her apartment building Kenneth turned to her.

"Would it be okay if I saw you to your door?" Simone thought for a brief moment, before nodding her head as she directed him to the entrance into the underground garage instead of the main entrance. She handed him her access key as pulled up to the gate.

He looked over at her and grinned, "Fancy."

"Oh whatever." She laughed. As they entered through the gate, Kenneth navigated his car around a few corners before pulling into a parking spot near the elevator.

Shutting off the engine Kenneth quickly got out of the car before walking around to open the passenger door. As they headed to the elevator he easily spotted her matching Audi S7. He also noticed the other four Audi models.

"Do they belong to you as well?" He asked.

Smiling she said, "Yes and no." She laughed at his confused expression. "Well you already know the S7 is mine. The S8 and Q5 are mine as well, however when in them I'm usually being driven by Charles. The A5 and S5 belong to Charles and Gladys my housekeeper. Kenneth let out a low whistle, "Fancy." They both cracked up laughing as they entered the elevator. Swiping her access card across the reader, Simone pushed the button for the Penthouse. She didn't need to look at him to know that once again that boyish smile was once again present on his face. She couldn't stop the smile that spread across her own.

Entering the foyer, Kenneth took notice of the paintings that graced the stark white walls. They were similar to the ones she had displayed in her office.

"These paintings are beautiful. You have similar ones in your office right?"

"Yes." She replied as she walked around to where he stood admiring one specific painting. She came and stood beside him.

"I like them. Abstract art is one of my favorite mediums. Who is the artist?" Simone smiled as she leaned towards one of them, her finger outstretched as she pointed to the signature at the bottom. Having signed off on several documents he had seen, Kenneth recognized her signature immediately. Turning to her, his eyes widened in amazement. "You...you painted this?" Her smile widened as she nodded her head.

For once he was lost for words as he once again gazed upon the beautiful painting.

Finally breaking the silence, Kenneth turned to face her. "You really are full of surprises." Simone lowered her head shyly. Placing his index finger under her chin, he slowly raised her head forcing her to look him in the eye.

"Thank you for joining me for dinner tonight. I had a wonderful time." Leaning in, Simone's breath caught in her throat as he softly kissed her cheek. "I'll see you in the morning." With that he turned and headed back towards the elevator.

Finally able to find words Simone stopped him as he pushed the call button for the elevator. Reaching into her pocket she held out the access card.

"Here, you'll need this to get out." Kenneth smiled at her as he entered the elevator. "How will you get out in the morning?"

She laughed, "I have extra. You can hold on to that one." She replied winking at him as the doors closed.

Chapter 18

Two weeks later

Two weeks had gone by since the graduation and their impromptu dinner. Two weeks since Kenneth had become more entranced by her. And two weeks— since the feel of her soft skin against his lips, caused a slow burning fire within him.

With his new intern starting last week, as well as the new developments he was working on, Kenneth had been very busy. He couldn't believe that in a week he will have been at BC Inc. for a month already; so much had happened and changed. Simone had been out of the office twice on out of town business meetings. Apart from their weekly marketing meeting last week, he hadn't seen her. He longed to spend more one on one time with her but forced himself to be patient. They had been communicating over the phone regularly since that night which helped. Their connection continued to grow stronger, but they still maintained a professional demeanor and certain degree of distance in the office. She was still his boss after all.

Walking into the kitchen to fix a cup of coffee and toast the bagel he'd brought for breakfast before starting his day, Kenneth smiled upon seeing Denise.

"I keep forgetting that you are the only other person who manages to beat me in most mornings."

Denise smiled as she turned to face him, still stirring her coffee.

"Good Morning to you too." Since his initial start, they had met for lunch a few times when their schedules permitted it. She really had been a great help in assisting him in getting settled within the company.

"How was your weekend? Did you and your husband enjoy the game Saturday night?" As a thank you for all of her help, Kenneth had given them two of his season tickets. "Yes, thanks again for them, it was really fun. We had such a great time."

"Anytime. Just let me know whenever you want to go. I can't always make it so at least this way they won't go to waste."

"Okay, I will definitely keep that in mind. Busy day for you today?"

"No, today should be pretty straightforward."

"That's good." Glancing at her watch Denise noticed the time. "Oh I have to get going. Simone has a conference meeting in twenty minutes."

"Well you better get to it." He teased.

"Later silly." She laughed as she headed out of the kitchen.

"Later."

Heading back to his office, coffee and bagel in hand, he suddenly heard his phone go off signaling that he had a message, just as he reached his door. Juggling the bagel atop his coffee he pulled his phone out of his pocket. It was from Denise.

I heard the "boss" was looking for you. Someone is running late today?

He chuckled slightly as he typed out a reply as he walked in, his head down.

Well thankfully you can vouch for me.

Just as he hit send, a voice stopped him in his tracks.

"Well well, where's mine?" As he slowly looked up, there Simone sat behind his desk, her head resting in her hand with a mischievous smile on her face. He instantly smiled. "This is a surprise," he began as he closed his door. "But I'll be sure to remember next time." Walking around his desk, he placed his food, coffee and briefcase down as she turned the chair to face him. The smoldering look in his eyes as he looked down at her was enough to make her heart flutter and her thighs to clench.

"To what do I owe this pleasure? I just ran into Denise in the kitchen and she had to rush off to prepare for your meeting in," he paused looking at his watch, "about fifteen minutes."

Glancing at her watch she eased out of his chair and seductively approached him coming to a stop in front of him. "I'm the boss remember. Besides, there was something more important that needed to be addressed. Something that is about two weeks overdue."

With only mere inches between them she reached up, placing her arms around his neck. Of their own violation, his arms wrapped securely around her slim waist, pulling her flush against his toned body as he asked, "Oh really? And what might that be?" No more words were needed as Simone boldly raised her head as he simultaneously lowered his. The instant their lips met, the fire that had merely simmered, erupted with such a force. Kenneth couldn't believe what was happening was actually happening, in his office, an act that Simone initiated. The kiss was both soft and powerful and for them both, long overdue, yet right on time. He hadn't expected her body to fit his so perfectly, or for her to feel so good in his arms. His hands began to unconsciously roam her curvy figure, slowly sliding them down her back until he reached and began caressing her ample backside. Simone let out a soft moan in response to his actions, immediately granting his probing tongue access to her sweet mouth. Kenneth sighed in satisfaction.

This went on for several moments until, as if it suddenly dawned on her where they were and where she needed to be, Simone reluctantly pulled away, easing out of his embrace. Kenneth was speechless. Just as well, he had slowly begun to find it difficult to keep himself, particular his lower self in check.

Simone just smiled as she backed away from him and headed towards the door. Placing her hand on the doorknob, she looked back at him, "See you later." And just like that she was gone.

For the rest of the day Kenneth found it hard to focus on anything work related. His mind constantly wondered to what happened this morning. He had to force himself to stay focused, working nonstop. He had even worked through his lunch break. Looking at the clock, he was surprised to see that it was almost time to knock off. Leaning back in his chair, he turned to look out the window becoming deep in thought. *What happens now?*

Simone didn't fear much different as she sat at her desk, lost in thought. After leaving Kenneth's office, her day had been nonstop since this morning. One meeting ran into another and another, leaving her fortunately or unfortunately, little to no time to reflect on her actions this morning. She had no idea what made her do it; it was as if she was acting on pure instinct. For the past two weeks her mind would constantly drift back to the softness of his lips as they touched her cheek. And all she knew was that she wanted no needed to feel them again. She had no idea where this was headed or what was happening. They hadn't had a chance to speak at all, all day.

As if the universe was suddenly working in her favor, her internal line rang. Turning back to face her desk, she reached over to answer it.

"Simone Caines."

"Have dinner with me tonight." Simone had agreed with no hesitation.

Chapter 19

Gladys was in the kitchen tidying up when Simone entered the main foyer of her penthouse apartment dressed and ready to go at six forty-five. Kenneth had just called to let her know he would be there in about ten minutes. Gladys had just placed her homemade apple turnovers into the oven. She smiled affectionately at Simone who was fussing with her outfit. She looked amazing as usual but Gladys knew well enough that she was doing this due to nerves. "You look fine Simone." she assured her. Simone had been so preoccupied she hadn't noticed her until just then. Kenneth had told her to dress fairly casual, so she had decided on a pair of black fitted jeans, a white designer tee with the word "Queen" on the front and an army green blazer. After work she had booked a last minute hair appointment. She'd had it washed, blow-dried and flat pressed.

"Thank you Gladys." She smiled at her before glancing at her watch. It was time for her to head downstairs.

"Do you and Charles have any plans tonight?"

"Yup. We're actually going to see a movie and then probably grab something to eat after."

"Oh sounds like fun. Well I hope you guys have a good time. See you."

"You as well."

Just as Simone had entered the lobby, Kenneth pulled up. He watched, mesmerized as she strolled to towards him. Even in somewhat casual attire she was stunning. He also noticed that for the first time since meeting her, she wore her hair out. It was longer than he would've expected since she always had it pulled back and tucked into a neat bun. Tonight instead, she wore it straight. He openly admired how her silky black tresses now hung loosely down her back. The bellman opened the door for her and she slid into the passenger seat. She smiled instantly at him. This time he couldn't care less about being caught staring.

"Like what you see Mr. Daniels?" she asked. Without answering he leaned in and kissed her. Now that he seemed to have open access to her full kissable lips, he planned on taking advantage of every opportunity. "Does that answer your question?" His kiss had left her momentarily speechless. She blushed and smiled in response. Kenneth laughed out loud as he pulled off onto the street.

Twenty minutes later he pulled up to the restaurant. Hopping out he handed the keys to the valet who seemed to light up at the opportunity to drive his car. Walking around to Simone's door he held her hand as he helped her out. Being that it was Friday night the place was rather crowded, but Kenneth had called and made a reservation early enough and had managed to secure a corner booth for them. As they took their seats, this time he chose to sit beside Simone instead of across from her.

"I'm glad you accepted my dinner invite. I know it was last minute," he said after they had placed their drink orders.

"I was glad to," she replied, wondering if she should be the one who brought up what happened this morning.

"How did the rest of your day go?" she continued on, "we didn't get a chance to speak after…" her voice trailed off, letting the words unspoken hang in the air.

He looked her straight in the eyes as he spoke, turning serious. "Simone, what happened this morning caught me by surprise but it was amazing. You're a smart woman so I'm sure you haven't been oblivious to the connection between us. I've wanted to take things further with you and get to know you better on a deeper level. I'm a patient man who knows what he wants, but with the obvious dynamics of our situation, I couldn't afford to rush things until you were okay with it." Simone looked at him for a long while before responding.

"I'll admit I did try and deny what I had been feeling for obvious and not so obvious reasons. I'm your boss and have never fraternized or entertained anyone I've worked with or who works for me. But you, you were different. You showed me different, your approach was different. I was growing tired of fighting it. I would like however, to still maintain a certain level of—decorum at work. I would hate to have to write you up for inappropriate conduct," she joked. Kenneth laughed

"Of course, I understand and respect that. The obvious reasons I can definitely understand. What are the not so obvious reasons?" A flash of sadness appeared in her eyes before she quickly recovered. "I can't—don't want to get into that right now, okay? Let's just take it one day at a time and go from there. Is that all right?"

Kenneth had seen the sudden change in her mood, but because they were making progress he knew not to push it. He was just happy that she was there with him and was willing to try. He told her so. "That's fine Simone, as I said I'm a patient man and I'm just glad to have you here and that you're willing to try." He reached up and caressed her cheek before once again claiming her lips.

The waiter came and took their food orders as they settled in to an easy conversation, enjoying being in this moment and each other's company.

Chapter 20

After dinner, they had decided to take a drive around the downtown area, taking in the sights before arriving back on to Simone's street. Pulling up to her building he placed the car in park. Simone spoke first. "Would you like to come up for a bit? Have some coffee maybe? Gladys has also made her amazing apple turnovers and seeing as we skipped dessert and—Kenneth leaned over and gently kissed her on the lips, effectively halting her nervous rambling. "I'd love to." Pulling back out onto the street, he circled around and entered the underground garage. He smiled as he pulled out the access card she had given him weeks ago. Simone laughed.

Parking in one of the reserved guest spots, they got out and headed towards the elevator. As they walked past her cars Kenneth noticed that one of her spots were empty. "Very perceptive of you," she teased. "But yes, Charles and Gladys are out."

"Together?" Kenneth asked incredulously, causing Simone to laugh out loud at his expression. "Yes, they're an item." she stated simply and they both left it at that as they entered the elevator.

Walking into the main foyer, Kenneth was impressed. "Nice place."

"Thank you," she called over her shoulder as she placed her purse on the island in the kitchen. "How long have you been living here?" he asked as he walked over and took a seat on one of the bar stools as he watched her prepare the coffee.

"I've lived here for six years. I love it. It's my fortress in the sky." While the coffee brewed, she proceeded to warm up two of the turnovers. Kenneth watched her in fascination, enjoying seeing her in yet another element of her life. He knew deep down that there was so much more to be found out. He wondered to himself, what exactly was the cause of her drive and the vulnerability she had spoken of at the graduation? He also wondered if she would ever allow him in enough to express these experiences and fears to him. But for now, he was smart enough to know not to push her.

Once everything was ready, they settled into the great room on her large charcoal colored sectional in front of the huge floor to ceiling windows. "This view is amazing," Kenneth exclaimed. Before joining him, she walked over to a built in console on one of the walls. Pushing one of the many buttons, a fire was ignited instantly in the built in fireplace anchoring the room. Simone walked over and took a seat a little ways away from him. She had taken off her heels and walked barefoot over to where he sat, sinking into the soft suede material. "Why are you all the way over there? Kenneth asked in jest. "I won't bite," he said as a sly grin appeared on his face. Simone grinned at him as she moved closer, before slowly taking a sip of her coffee.

There was a companionable silence for a few minutes as they sat enjoying the coffee, view and each other's company.

"These smell really good," he said before breaking off a piece of the turnover and taking a bite. He closed his eyes as the freshness and flavors tickled his palate. Simone watched him. She sat mesmerized as his cushy, soft lips caressed his spoon as he eased the fluffy pastry off the end of it. He opened his eyes and caught Simone staring. She quickly diverted her eyes as she took another bite of her dessert. Kenneth just smiled. Another moment passed before Simone responded. "They're my favorite. Gladys would make them every day if I wanted, but that would be detrimental to my figure." They both laughed. Kenneth's eyes slowly perused said figure and found absolutely nothing wrong with it. He didn't comment but the look in his eyes showed his appreciation for her curves.

"Well they're delicious."

"I'll be sure to let her know that you approve," she said with a smirk.

The two of them continued talking as they finished off their dessert and coffee. Kenneth filled Simone in on his new intern's progress; he was coming along nicely and had the craziest sense of humor. Simone in turn briefed Kenneth on the new, substantial business moves she was planning. She had only shared these ideas with Barb and Denise and told him as such. He was pleasantly surprised and happy that she was deciding to share this with him. He told this to her.

"I must admit that I am a little surprised that you are deciding to share this with me." Simone smiled as she placed her now finished mug on the coffee table. Leaning back against the couch, she tucked her bare feet underneath her.

"Well there are still a lot of specifics that I'm leaving out," she paused slightly hesitating before deciding to be open with him. "But, after spending time with you in and specifically outside of work, it would be silly to deny the connection we've built. I do not have many people in my life that I trust or let in, but somehow, you've gotten me to lower my guard." Kenneth took a deep breath as her revelation both left him momentarily speechless and touched his heart in such a profound way. Simone panicked slightly at his reaction, wondering if she had shared too much. He was quiet for a moment, which further unnerved her, but then he smiled at her, immediately putting her at ease.

"You have no idea how glad I am to hear you say that," he reassured her. "I've been intrigued by you since the first day we met. But after being hired by you and then with Denise giving me a subtle yet fair warning to keep it professional," he chuckled slightly before continuing, I decided to do just that; well I tried to anyway." Simone just shook her head and smiled at what he'd said about Denise.

"Denise had told me about your little conversation after our final interview." Kenneth raised his brow in surprise.

"She did? I wasn't aware you two talked like that."

"Yes, she did. And yes we do, she is my best friend after all."

"She is?' Kenneth was really shocked at this revelation, but now looking back on everything it did make sense. Denise was the only person he had noticed who seemed to not be intimidated by Simone. It also explained why he would see Denise with Simone more than anyone else. Of course he initially assumed this was because she was simply her assistant.

Simone laughed out loud at his response.

"We've been friends since middle school. I met her my first day after I had transferred there. Our lockers were next to each other and while I was having difficulty opening mine, she had helped me. Coincidentally, we ended up having the majority of the same classes. We've been best friends ever since."

Kenneth sat there listening to her, thoroughly enjoying hearing something from Simone's past. While he'd given her plenty of details about his upbringing and family, he had noticed that Simone didn't talk about her past or mention anything about family. He had wondered about this a few times but had never asked her.

Simone continued on, "She's actually the only person in my life who knows me that well." It had been a long, long time since Simone had come close to thinking, let alone talking about her life back then. There was something about him that made her open up without question. She felt the memories begin to creep in and slowly withdrew within. Wrapping her arms protectively around herself, she fought vehemently to ward off those thoughts.

Kenneth reached over took her hand. He held her smaller hand in his larger one for a few moments before asking, "Are you okay Simone?"

She took a moment before responding, allowing her rapidly beating heart to slow as his touch helped to ground her.

"I'm okay," she took a deep breath, "It's just that..." Kenneth stopped her.

"Simone, we don't have to talk about it right now. I can see that it is obviously difficult for you and we're having such a nice night. When the time is right and when you're ready, okay?" Simone looked at him a long moment. It wasn't so much that she felt as if she couldn't let him in. She was more worried that when he found out what troubles existed in her past that it would push him away. *But he isn't like him Simone. Just take it one day at a time.* Denise's words echoed in her mind from a conversation they had had earlier today after she had told her that they were going to dinner. Shaking off the bad feelings as she brought herself back into the moment, she smiled at him.

"Okay. Would you like a tour?" Kenneth returned her smile as he nodded. He forced himself not to focus on what could be the cause of the pain he saw as they stood. There was something about her showing him her vulnerability that spoke volumes to him. He knew in that moment that he couldn't walk away.

Chapter 21

After placing their dishes in the kitchen, Simone started off by showing him her office, which was just off of the great room.

"My office is over here," she said walking over and standing in the doorway.

"Not bad." He teased as he poked his head in. Kenneth took note of what looked to be a smaller, yet equally as extensive version of her office at work. As he turned around to follow Simone, he noticed a long hallway just off to the left of the great room which was in the opposite direction of where she was heading.

"What's down that way?" He'd asked, curious that they hadn't started in that direction. After picking up her heels she looked in the direction he'd asked about.

"Oh that's Charles and Gladys' living quarters. Initially it was sectioned off when they had both started working for me, giving them each their own separate lounging area. After they had become an item, the wall was knocked down to combine their spaces. There are two bedrooms, two baths and an office for each of them."

"Wow, that's pretty impressive."

"And to think you haven't even seen a quarter of this place." Simone chuckled as she walked towards a grand staircase. She rested her shoes down before stepping up on to the plush white carpet of the first step. Reaching the second level, she started by showing him the three guest bedrooms, each one equipped with its own bathroom. Next she showed him a fairly decent sized at-home gym. One that by his standards, was better than most he'd seen.

"This looks better than the gym I attend, which is a shame for what they charge."

Simone laughed as she responded, "Well you're welcome to come and use it anytime, and "she paused," at no charge of course. I work out at least four times a week. "

.

"Where do I sign up? I could use a new workout buddy." Kenneth joked.

Although the look in his eyes showed he would certainly and eagerly take her up on that offer. As he said this, thoughts of him hot and sweaty instantly popped into her mind. Shaking them off she hurriedly moved the tour along. Kenneth smiled slightly as he followed her down the hall.

Opening the door she continued on, "And next is the entertainment room." As they walked in, he let out a low whistle, impressed yet again. Kenneth had been expecting a usual TV room. When in fact Simone had a mini movie theater. With three rows of authentic red, cushiony leather movie theater type chairs that fully reclined, a jumbo movie screen and projector.

"Man this is something else. Do you come in here often?"

"Not so much. Charles uses it more than either myself or Gladys-- especially on Sundays." Simone rolled her eyes as she said this, but smiled nonetheless.

Kenneth laughed out loud. "Sounds about right." Turning to leave the room, Kenneth allowed Simone to walk out in front of him as he closed the door.

"Well that's it for up here. Seen enough yet?" Simone asked as they headed back towards the staircase.

"Nope I'm enjoying myself. Please continue madam." Reaching the landing she picked up her shoes as she guided him down another hallway in the opposite direction from where Gladys and Charles' quarters were. Kenneth reached over and eased the heels out of her hand.

"Allow me." he said as he winked at her.

"Thanks." she smiled in response.

The first room they passed was a fully stocked library, which doubled as a rec room. There was a smaller L-shaped sofa similar to the one in the great room off to the right. In the center of the room was a custom made pool table.

"Do you play? Or is that more for Charles' benefit." A smirk evident on his face, Simone smiled, "I play a little, but yes it is definitely used more by Charles."

"Is there any room that is specifically yours?" Kenneth asked as they walked out.

"Actually, there is. Your timing is spot on." Continuing down the hall Simone stopped outside of a large metal door. Placing her hand on the handle she slid the door open revealing her studio. Kenneth's eyes widened in amazement as they walked inside and he took it all in. On the right side of the room was a desk with papers, books and sketchpads spread atop its surface. A fair sized shelving unit stood behind it which had several containers filled with a variety of paints, brushes, various pens, markers, pencils, etc. as well as a vast variety of other art supplies.

On the left wall was a rack of sorts that was filled with different size canvases and sheets of drawing paper. At the back of the room, several drawings and paintings hung along the wall. A range of emotions displayed in each one; some of them containing poems written on top of an abstract background. In front of them at the back of the room there stood an art aisle, an unfinished canvas painting resting on it. Kenneth looked over at Simone who had also been quiet as she watched him as he perused the room.

"May I?" he asked cautiously. He didn't want to take it upon himself to go and take a closer look. She slowly nodded her head. Kenneth then proceeded to walk over and stand in front of it, gazing intently at it in silence. She had finished drawing and had just started to paint it. Even unfinished, to him it was still beautiful. She had drawn a humming bird drinking from a flower and what looked to be a small flowerbed with a small pool of water atop of the leaves. Simone, who had kept a few feet back, wondered what was going through his mind. She had never shown anyone her art. Other than Denise, who had known of Simone's talent from when they were kids. Gladys and Charles knew as well, but it had taken at least three years before she had shared this with even them. Kenneth who had stood there for what seemed like ages, finally turned to face her after taking in all of it again. "This is…beautiful. You are really talented."

"Thank you," she stated simply, for the way he now looked at her caused her heart to flutter. He walked back over to where she stood, coming to a stop in front of her. He slowly reached up and caressed her face before embracing her. "Thank you for showing me this." They stood this way for a while before she slowly withdrew from his embrace. Taking her hand they headed out, rounding the corner they came upon the door to Simone's master suite.

"Here we are the last stop on the tour."

"After you."

Chapter 22

Entering her bedroom Kenneth immediately took in the decor. The layout was simple, much like the rest of the apartment. Nevertheless, the modern feel and decor gave it a sophisticated and homey feel. It was one that fit Simone to a tee. An electric fireplace was built into the wall in the corner nook on one side of the room. A small leather love seat sat in front of it, giving the area a cozy feel. A padded, charcoal grey king sized platform bed set atop a black raised platform against the back main wall. Plush white carpets greeted him at the door, stretching across the length of the room that came to an end at the base of the floor to ceiling windows. Across the length of the far wall, they revealed yet another breathtaking view. Simone hadn't asked him to but he felt compelled to take his shoes off so as not to taint its pure appearance.

Walking towards him after placing her iPhone on the nightstand, Simone smiled at his actions as she noticed he still held her shoes in his hand.

"I can take those now," she said still smiling at him once she reached him. Returning her smile, he handed them to her. "My closet is over here." As she walked in, Simone flicked the switch, illuminating the massive walk in closet. Kenneth chuckled slightly as he shook his head.

"What's so funny?" Simone asked as she walked over and placed her heels in their designated spot. "I thought my mother and sister's closets were massive," Kenneth teased as he reentered her bedroom. Walking over to the large bay windows overlooking the south shore, he stood, quietly taking in the view. Exiting her closest Simone watched him for a moment, wondering what was going through his mind. She took advantage of this unguarded moment to take in the man who, out of nowhere, blew into her life.

She took in his freshly cut, close-cropped hair. Smiling to herself, she remembered how at dinner he had joked about how even as grown men, there was still that sense of excitement after getting a 'fresh clip'. His long lashes hovered above beautiful brown eyes, that at the moment she could not see but surely remembered the myriad of feelings they invoked within her when he looked at her. Her eyes became hooded as they came to rest on his soft full lips. A heat instantly spread through her core at the mere memory of how they felt pressed against hers.

"You know," she began as she came to stand next to him, joining him at the window, "In the six years that I've lived here, you're the only man who has been in here."

He stood there for what seemed like an eternity before slowly turning his head to face her. The look on his face was unreadable but the smoldering look in his eyes—as he gazed upon the woman who was slowly but surely capturing his heart—was not. The look of desire in his eyes caused a rush of heat to explode between her thighs, immediately causing her lace thong to become wet.

As he reached up, cupping her face with both hands, he placed a kiss on her forehead. Simone closed her eyes at its sincerity. He softly kissed first her right temple and then her left, as he ran his hands down her neck, along her shoulders and slowly down her back, coming to a stop at her lower back. Of their own accord, her arms reached up and wrapped around his neck as he pulled her close. Gazing intently into her eyes, he slowly lowered his head as she raised hers and kissed her deeply. Running his tongue along her bottom lip, quietly requesting entry into her sweet mouth. Simone obliged as a slight moan escaped her mouth as his tongue met hers and set her body aflame. As their kiss deepened another breathless moan escaped her mouth causing his lower body to stir, making its presence known.

To his surprise, rather than being startled, Simone squirmed to get closer. Her hand began caressing his neck before pulling him closer. Sliding his hands down her back and then lower, cupping her backside, Kenneth lifted Simone effortlessly into his arms and walked them to the bed. Lowering them down onto the soft mattress, he covered her body with his as they continued to kiss passionately. Running his hand lightly over her body, gently squeezing her ample breast before continuing his sensual journey along her curves. Fully enthralled in the moment, Simone could feel her guard lowering as he caressed her, his kisses driving her crazy. Eager to feel and caress her soft skin, his hand reached for the hem of her tee. His strong, capable fingers had just begun to caress her stomach when Simone's eyes flew open.

"Stop, wait...I can't do this," placing her hands on his shoulders, halting any further progression.

I hope he didn't see it. This thought raced through her mind as she quickly readjusted her shirt.

Hearing the panic in her voice, Kenneth immediately raised himself up. Leaning back on his heels he tried to make sense of her abrupt change in mood.

"I'm sorry if I moved too fast," he said apologetically,

Even though he knew there was no denying the instant reaction he had seen and felt from her body.

What had happened?

Simone took in his sad expression and felt bad, but she had panicked. Her reaction was automatic.

"You didn't move to fast, I'm just...I'm just realizing it would be better for me if we waited just a little longer." She dropped her gaze, as he looked at her, not able to look him in the eyes. Kenneth looked at her a long moment before moving off the bed.

Simone looked up abruptly. "Where are you going?"

"I thought you may have wanted me to leave." he replied, easing his hands into his pockets. Rising up on her knees, moving in front of him she wrapped her arms around his waist, resting her head against his now slow beating heart—its steady rhythm soothing her warring mind.

"I'm sorry." He smiled as he embraced her. Placing his index finger under her chin, he raised her head to look at him.

"Don't be Simone, what just happened was amazing. When it's meant for it to go any further it will, okay?"

"Okay," she paused, "Do you have any plans tomorrow?"

"Nothing that I can think of at the moment. Do you want me to stay?"

"Would you mind?"

He leaned down and placed a soft kiss on her lips before responding, "Not at all."

A few minutes later, after changing into a long silk nightgown, Simone crawled back into bed. Kenneth who had discarded his jeans and now stood in a black under vest and black boxer briefs climbed in next to her, taking her in his arms. The two talked for the next twenty or so minutes before Simone fell fast asleep. Kenneth however, laid there deep in thought for a while before joining her.

Chapter 23

The next morning, a fully dressed Kenneth walked into the kitchen just as Simone had finished up with a business call on her cellphone. After hanging up she placed a freshly brewed cup of coffee on the island in front of him. "Thank you," he smiled taking a seat on one of the bar stools as he graciously accepted the cup. Picking up her mug, Simone leaned against the counter. Theirs was a companionable silence as they both enjoyed the freshly brewed cup of coffee.

Placing his mug down Kenneth spoke first, "Are you hungry?"

Just as Simone went to answer him, her phone rang again.

"Sorry, one minute." He half expected her to step out of the room; surprisingly she came around and sat on the stool next to him.

She listened to the caller briefly. "I want the specifics emailed to me within the next two hours," with that, she ended the call.

Her straightforward business manner caused a slight smile to spread across his face.

"Sorry about that. You were saying?"

"Not a problem. I was just wondering if you were hungry and wanted to go and grab some breakfast."

She glanced at her watch before responding,

"I'm sorry, but I can't. I wouldn't have minded but I have two conference calls back to back."

Kenneth, with his easygoing nature, was a tad disappointed but he understood.

"That's okay. I understand you're a busy lady. Do you have to go into the office today?"

"Actually no, I usually work from home on the weekends. Gladys has fixed an egg and spinach frittata and cinnamon rolls if you wanted to eat here," she offered up. Even though she had work to do, surprisingly she wasn't ready to have him leave her company.

"Sure I'd love some," he eagerly accepted, not ready to depart from her either.

"Okay." Smiling, she proceeded to busy herself with preparing their plates. When everything was sorted, refilling their mugs, the two settled into an easy conversation as they enjoyed their breakfast. Once they'd finished eating, Kenneth rose from his seat. Collecting their plates, he walked around the island and placed them by the sink. He was about to start washing them but Simone stopped him.

"You don't have to worry about washing those. I'll load them in the dishwasher and Gladys will get to them after she finishes her prep for the week."

Walking back around the island, he came to a stop in front of her placing a kiss on her cheek.

"Breakfast was delicious, thank you." Taking her hand, slowly pulling her up from the stool, he wrapped her securely in his arms.

"You're welcome," she said returning his embrace. They stayed this way for a moment before he lowered his head and claimed her lips.

I'm starting to believe I could stay this way for—just then, the ringing of her cellphone broke through the moment. Smiling against her mouth, he reluctantly let her go.

Reaching for her phone she glanced at the screen before answering.

"Yes Barb," she was only half listening however, unable to take her eyes off of him as he walked over to retrieve his jacket.

"We'll discuss the needed changes during the call. Send me the specifics so I'll have them beforehand." She hung up and walked over towards the elevator where he now stood. Pushing the button as she approached, he reached up and gently caressed her face.

"Call me later." Leaning down, he kissed her softly before stepping inside.

Chapter 24

After the doors had closed, Simone let out a sigh as she walked back into the main foyer. At this time both Charles and Gladys were now in the kitchen. She took a seat next to Charles, who was reading the paper as Gladys was starting preparations for lunch; she usually kept it simple on weekends.

"Morning Gladys, Charles."

"Miss Caines," Charles replied, his eyes never leaving the sports section.

"Any special request for lunch today dear?" She asked in way of greeting as Simone settled in.

"I'm easy Gladys, whatever you decide is fine."

"Okay. Will you be working from home today?" she asked as she walked over and placed freshly poured cups of coffee in front of both Simone and Charles. Grabbing her cup, Simone rose from her chair and headed towards her office.

"Yes I have two conference calls scheduled for today," she called over her shoulder.

Simone smiled to herself as she entered her office. Both Gladys and Charles were early risers, so she knew that if they hadn't seen Kenneth leaving they had at least heard them in the kitchen earlier. Around this time, Gladys would have completed her lunch and dinner prep and both she and Charles would spend time elsewhere in the apartment- usually the rooftop garden. Neither of them would address it nor ask Simone about it until she made it known.

Secretly, they were both happy about what was building between Simone and Kenneth. Since they had both started working for and living with Simone, no man had spent time there. Charles, who was always an excellent judge of character, had immediately taken a liking to Kenneth that first day when they met outside of BC Inc. Knowing Simone hadn't and wouldn't, he had shared the encounter with Gladys. Both of them knew all too well the darkness with which Simone kept buried deep. Having grown fond of such an amazing young woman, they only wanted the best for her.

Kenneth's mind was preoccupied as he pulled up to the large wrought iron gate outside of his mother's estate. She had called him just as he had left Simone's place and asked if he wanted to come by for lunch. He had nothing else planned this weekend and was grateful for the invite. He'd sat there for almost two minutes before realizing he hadn't punched in the access code. Reaching his arm out of the window he entered the numbers, the gate opening in seconds. Once the gate opened, he eased his car up the long, graveled driveway leading up to the estate. Pulling his car into the circular driveway, he smiled as his mother stood waiting for him on the front step. He quickly exited the car and bound up the stairs, enveloping his favorite person in the world in a huge bear hug.

"Hello son!"

"Hey mom."

"I'm so glad you were able to come by on such short notice." She linked her arm with his as they headed inside.

"I was actually on my way home with no plans, so thank you. I'm starving anyway, please tell me the food is ready!" Janice laughed as they entered the kitchen.

Minutes later they sat enjoying their meal, after they had decided to dine outside on the patio. Janice smiled at her youngest as he dug into his plate with gusto. His mother had made his favorite: her famous spicy chili and homemade cornbread.

"You know, Kendra isn't going to magically appear and try and beat you at finishing first or steal your food," she teased paying reference to the endless although good-natured competitiveness between her children. Kenneth smiled in response as he continued demolishing his plate. Finally placing his spoon down, he leaned back in his chair.

"Where are Kendra and the little rugrats anyway?" He queried about his niece and nephew who were usually spending the weekend with their grandmother.

"Thomas' parents and I alternated weekends. They have a function next week and won't be able to have them. Besides,

James is back in town from his most recent business trip and would like to treat me to dinner," she replied. James was a wonderful man who came into their lives ten years after Kenneth's father had passed away when he and Kendra were only three and seven. Kenneth smiled at this statement for his mother barely needed any reason to eat out.

"Sure mom, I'm sure that's the reason you're eating out. What are Kendra and Thomas up to since they aren't here?"

"They took an impromptu weekend trip to New York. Which reminds me actually, since everyone is away, Sunday dinner is postponed until next week if you're still free."

"Even if I had plans, you know I'd cancel them in a minute for my favorite girl," he winked at his mother, placing a kiss on her cheek before standing.

Grabbing their bowls he headed inside. He returned a few minutes after, carrying a tray holding two glasses of ice and a pitcher filled with freshly squeezed lemonade.

"So what's been going on with you son? You've been so busy lately."

"The new job has definitely kept me busy, but it's been great. The new intern, Joshua started a couple of weeks ago. He's very perceptive and intelligent. I'm positive Simone will keep him on once his internship is complete."

Janice, who didn't miss much, casually raised an eyebrow at the use of his boss's first name. She hid her smile behind taking a sip of her beverage. She knew better then to press him about it. One of the things she valued about their relationship, her relationship with both her children, was that they had no secrets from each other and were open about everything. Kendra was very expressive and often times had to be reeled in. Kenneth on the other hand, was like his father; he took time to mull things over before talking about it.

Kenneth stayed at his mother's for the better part of two hours, catching each other up on what they'd missed in each other's lives. Walking out to his car, Kenneth turned and hugged his mother.

"This was great mom. Thanks again for lunch."

"Anytime son. Oh before I forget, check your mail when you get home. The invite for my 'big sendoff' in two weeks should have arrived. They were sent out this week." She laughed as he rolled his eyes, knowing the formality of sending out invites was Kendra's idea.

"Alright mom. I'll give you a call tomorrow. I love you."

"Love you too baby. Drive safely."

As he drove towards the gate, he couldn't help but smile at the great time he'd had. As he waited for the gate to open his cellphone rang, his smile widened instantly.

"Good evening, Mr. Daniels." Simone's sultry tone filtered through his hand held speakers.

Chapter 25

Walking through the revolving doors, Simone found herself in an exceptionally chipper mood. She didn't see Kenneth again for the rest of the weekend, but they'd spent hours talking over the phone, a combination of personal and business. The business was mainly due to their weekly meeting at 11:00am this morning. Her bed had felt strangely empty since having shared it with him. As she waited for the elevator to arrive, she closed her eyes briefly, her body instantly warming at the memory. *Those eyes, as they bore into hers as he—*

The elevator dinged, breaking her out of her daydream. Before stepping into the elevator, she looked down as she searched for her swipe inside of her purse. As she turned to face the panel she gasped as she came face to face with...those eyes.

"Good Morning Miss Caines." Kenneth's professional and business like greeting belied the fiery look in his eyes.

"Good Morning Mr. Daniels."

Recovering quickly as a few other employees entered the elevator, she stepped aside to make room. Kenneth quickly moved to stand beside her. His scent and presence were driving her crazy. His thoughts were equally similar, he found it difficult to concentrate on what one of his colleagues was saying as he swore he could feel the heat radiating from her body. Arriving at their offices, everyone piled out of the elevator and headed to their respective departments.

Simone made a beeline in the direction of her office. Today was going to be a long day and she needed to have her wits about her. Watching her scurry away from him, Kenneth just smiled as he continued to his office.

"Good Morning Simone."

"Morning Denise. My office in five minutes." Grabbing the notices she held out, Simone breezed past her, never breaking stride as she entered her office. Walking into the office five minutes later, after placing a fresh cup of coffee on the desk, Denise took a seat in one of the chairs adjacent to Simone's desk.

Waiting patiently as Simone finished up a phone call, Denise busied herself by looking over her daily agenda. Occasionally she would glance at her boss as she conversed with the person on the phone. She noted that Simone seemed a little distracted today and that wasn't like her. Closing the cover on her iPad, crossing her legs, she leaned back in the chair and—even though she knew it annoyed Simone greatly—she began to observe her closely, speculatively. Placing the phone back in its cradle, Simone who was already on edge cut Denise a look as she finally reached for her mug. "You know that I hate it when you do that," she stated as she brought the mug to her lips.

"True, but you love me so that's why you put up with my ways," Denise responded unbothered. Rolling her eyes Simone sat back in her chair taking a sip. "Shoot!" Simone exclaimed as the heat from the mug burned her lip. Simultaneously, a few drops of the coffee spilled onto her blazer.

"I'm sorry Simone! I apologize if I made it too hot!" Denise sat up in her chair instantly.

"It's not your fault Denise. The temperature of the coffee is fine; the lip of the mug was hotter than expected.

Rising from her seat she quickly took off her jacket, rushing into her bathroom to get the stain out. Her movements had been quick, but not fast enough for Denise's perceptive eyes—pokey eyes as Simone called them—to miss the obvious passion mark that could be seen on her right shoulder due to her wearing a sleeveless silk grey shell underneath. Denise once again sat back against the soft leather of her seat, crossing her legs and folding her arms. She didn't even try to hide the enormous grin on her face. Minutes later Simone walked out of the bathroom placing her blazer on the back of her chair before taking a seat.

"Okay so today—" she stopped suddenly as she looked in Denise's direction and noticed the huge grin on her face. Sitting back in her chair she crossed her arms, a frown marring her face.

Denise said nothing but continued to stare at her, her smile growing larger.

"What is so funny?" she asked, her patience growing thin.

"How was your weekend?" Denise asked casually.

It was a simple question, but it was one that instantly caused Simone to clench her thighs, as she grew warm at the memories. She tried to appear calm even as she could feel a flush creeping up her neck.

"It was fine."

"*Do* anything special?"

"No…not really. Went to dinner Friday night is all. I did tell you this already."

Denise eyed her best friend carefully as she thought back to the conversation they'd had on Friday. Even though Simone had accepted immediately, she was still hesitant. Denise encouraged her to go. Simone looked away and began typing on her keyboard. Denise continued to stare, and then placing her hand over her mouth, she gasped. "Ooh, you gave him some didn't you??" Denise queried.

It just now dawned on her that her phone calls had gone unanswered later that evening, when she had called to find out how the dinner went. Simone jumped up and looked towards her open office door. It was an irrational act since her office was far enough away from the rest of the other departments.

"Be quiet Denise!"

Just as Denise was about to start quizzing her, one of the receptionist voices boomed over the intercom on Simone's desk.

"Miss Caines they are ready for you in conference room one."

Pushing the button she replied, "I'll be there momentarily."

"Saved by the bell." Denise smiled as she stood, gathering her belongings. Simone began doing the same, grateful for the distraction because she was not in the mood to be grilled by Denise. As she turned to head back to her office, Denise stopped as she noticed Simone about to head out without her blazer.

Simone looked at her, "Did you forget something?" she glanced at her desk.

Laughing slightly Denise turned and continued towards the door. "No, but you did. I'd reconsider not wearing your blazer. Unless you want everyone to see that hickey on your shoulder," she stated casually without turning around. "Let's do lunch."

With that she was out the door. Snatching her blazer from the back of her chair, Simone couldn't help but smile at Denise as she too headed out of her office to begin her day. As much as she got under her skin, Simone couldn't imagine her life without her.

Chapter 26

The conversation had been fairly casual as Simone and Denise sat eating their lunch at the conference table in Simone's office. It had been raining all morning and neither woman wanted to weather the rain. Needing to familiarize and go over the notes Kenneth had sent her in preparation for their weekly meeting, Simone alternated between scrolling through the notes on her iPad and eating the soup and sandwich Denise had grabbed for her from the cafeteria on the 10th floor. Again she was impressed with his thoroughness and innovativeness, she shared this with Denise.

"And you still haven't shared with him the prospect of him heading up his own company in about seven months? He'll have been here for about a year at that point right?" she queried, taking the iPad Simone handed her and reading over it for herself. Simone nodded her head.

"Well I did mention to him that there were expansions that I was working on. But no, I left that detail out. I want it to be further along and out of the development stage before that's revealed. And this way, Joshua, his intern will have completed the program and can be signed on as well." she explained. Simone had been thoroughly impressed with Joshua's progress as well. The final decision would be up to Kenneth of course, but she would gladly support it. Simone smiled inwardly as she thought of the other expansion she had planned for. She had decided to branch out into publishing as well. This too would be a welcomed challenge; one that she would be handing over to Denise. It was the least she could do for someone who had been there for her through everything. And someone who, armed with an MBA and masters in English, had graciously become Simone's assistant when she could have found employment elsewhere.

Placing the iPad down, Denise focused all of her attention on her friend and boss. She felt she had given her enough of a grace period before grilling her about what had transpired between her and one Kenneth Daniels.

"So," she began. Simone groaned in response. She had hoped Denise had forgotten or would at least let it go; of course she knew better. With a sigh, she reared back in her chair and conceded to her fate—Denise never gave up.

"I take it you and Mr. Daniels had an amazing time Friday night," she stated, a sly smile on her face.

"Yes, actually we did."

"Do tell." Simone proceeded to fill her in on the night's events-- dinner, inviting him up, the tour, her near emotional meltdown."

Denise's heart clenched at the mention of that last bit. It was part of the reason she had encouraged Simone to go out with Kenneth in the first place. Her friend deserved someone who could make her happy and who she could trust. She deserved to be with a person who, after all this time, could finally remove the hurt and would not look at Simone any different. But, Simone had to be willing to let him in.

"You still don't have any idea what could be prompting your nightmares again or the flashbacks?"

"Dr. Phillips asked the same question and I told her I have no idea either. It's difficult and frustrating though, because I know part of me is blocking out whatever it is deliberately. I'm not trying to revisit that or have those memories consuming my life."

"I know Simone, especially because you seemed to be making such progress." Not wanting to bring Simone down she changed the subject.

"Anyways. So after the tour, who seduced who?" she asked, taking joy in the flustered look on Simone's face.

"You get on my nerves, you know that!" They both cracked up laughing.

Then Simone turned serious, as she told Denise about how close they'd gotten before she panicked and backed out. Her voice trailed off as her mind drifted back.

"How did he react? Did he see the scar? I mean to hear you tell it he had you floating on cloud nine. What made you stop?"

"No he didn't see it. And I'm not sure, all I know was as soon as I felt his hand there I panicked. I thought he would leave after that, but he stayed. He was compassionate, understanding…" she sighed, "Honestly sometimes I feel as if he's too good to be true. Afterward, we just laid there talking about anything and then I fell asleep. I can't remember the last time I slept so soundly."

Denise smiled at the dreamy expression on her best friend's face. She was happy for her and hoped they would have the happy ending, well the beginning she knew she deserved. Glancing at her watch, she noticed her lunch break was almost up and she had to prepare the conference room for the remainder of the meetings this afternoon. Standing she walked over to Simone who had stood as well and hugged her, Simone returned her embrace.

"Well you know I'm happy for you girl. And, as I said before, just take it one day at a time. He's a good man; we both know you wouldn't have let him in this much if he weren't. Now, let me go start setting up before my boss tries to throw a tantrum. " With that she grabbed her phone off the table and left the office. Simone rolled her eyes even as she smiled in response.

Chapter 27

Later that day

Throughout the course of the day Kenneth hadn't been able to get Simone off of his mind. They hadn't spoken or interacted at all today and now he had to sit in close proximity to her and act completely neutral. As the meeting came to an end Kenneth mentally gave himself a pat on the back. He and his team had once again superseded not only his expectations but it appeared they had also done so for Simone's. He was also pleased that he had managed to keep himself in check throughout his entire presentation.

"Okay that'll be all for today, well done everyone. I am very pleased with the progress we're making." Simone said to the group, concluding the meeting. Effectively being dismissed, those in attendance gathered their belongings and filed out of the room. As he collected the outlines he'd handed out from his colleagues, Kenneth stole a glance at Simone who now had her head down, focusing on reading something on her iPad. *I'll give her a call later.* He said to himself a little disappointed. Picking up his folder he headed for the door.

"Mr. Daniels, may I have a word with you please." Simone said to his retreating back.

Her voice, even though professional, still filtered through his senses. He turned back around to face her.

"Close the door," she instructed in a tone that made him weak in the knees. Closing the door to, he swallowed hard as he watched her rise from her seat and slowly walk towards him.

"How was your day Mr. Daniels?

"My day was okay. How was yours?"

"Fine."

"That's good."

"Has it been busy day for you or have you just not missed me?" There was a wisp of a smile on her face as she sat on the edge of the conference table. His eyes immediately darkening with desire, that sinful grin on his face, he took a couple of steps towards her.

"I could ask you the same thing Miss Caines."

Reaching up, he lightly ran his index finger along her bottom lip.

"I've missed these," the look in his eyes caused a moistening in her panties and left her momentarily speechless. "May I?"

Still unable to speak, Simone slowly nodded her head. Softly caressing her face he lowered his head, claiming her lips. After a few moments, the ringing of her cellphone interrupted them. Kenneth begrudgingly pulled away suddenly remembering they were standing in the middle of a conference room that almost everyone had access to.

"Yes, I'll be there shortly," she said to Denise who informed her that everything was set up for her next meeting. "I'm sorry I have to go." She offered up a weak smile but Kenneth took note of the sadness in her eyes. This moved him deeply.

"There's no need to apologize Simone. I understand. Are you free this evening?"

"I have a business dinner I have to attend and then I'm catching a 9:30pm flight to New York. I have business meetings there tomorrow until Thursday and then I should be back by Friday afternoon."

"Okay world traveler." Kenneth joked in an attempt to break the somber mood. It worked. Simone laughed.

"I have no plans on Friday night, would that work for you?"

"Sure that's perfect, dinner at my place sound ok?" he replied pulling her into his arms.

"That sounds perfect. You're cooking?" she asked skeptically.

Kenneth laughed at her quizzical facial expression.

"I guess you'll just have to wait and see. I'm going to miss you."

She placed a soft, quick kiss on his lips before responding, 'I'm going to miss you too." Releasing her, he allowed her to leave out first before following.

Chapter 28

The rest of the week went by in a bit of a haze as Kenneth eagerly awaited Friday's arrival. Remembering Simone mentioning that she loved shrimp, Kenneth had prepared a shrimp scampi. He'd paired it with caesar salad and garlic bread. For dessert he kept it simple, settling on vanilla ice cream and apple turnovers. He was unexpectedly nervous. He wanted everything to go perfectly since he planned to ask her to join him for Sunday dinner at his mother's; he only hoped she'd accept. Twenty minutes later his doorbell rang. Simone had decided to have Charles drop her off rather than Kenneth picking her up from the airport. She had wanted to go home and freshen up after traveling. Kenneth had dressed in brown slacks and a beige button up shirt. Walking to the door, he looked through the peephole and what he saw instantly aroused him. He took a deep breath to calm his ardor. Opening the door, his smile was instant.

As she stepped through the door, he placed a soft kiss on her cheek before closing the door behind her.

He offered to take her coat. She had donned a form fitting black all in one romper. She had worn her hair out once again. The thick tresses hung almost halfway down her back, covering her open back.

"Simone you look beautiful." Smiling, she said, "Thank you Mr. Daniels. You're looking rather handsome yourself. She held out a bottle of white wine, hoping it went well with whatever he had made; he still hadn't told her.

He gladly accepted it, pleased at her selection. "Thank you, but you didn't have to. This will go perfectly with dinner."

"Speaking of, something smells wonderful."

"I told you I could cook."

Taking her by the hand he led her down the hallway and into the dining room. He had placed a variety of candles around the room and began lighting them as Simone took in the beautiful setting. The place setting was simple yet elegant, her eyes settling on a huge bouquet of peach colored roses which he used as centerpiece. As he finished lighting the last candle, he came up behind Simone and wrapped his arms around her as she stood in front of the windows overlooking the pool and backyard. She leaned back against him, once again feeling safe and secure in his arms.

"Are you ready to eat pretty lady?" he asked as he nuzzled her neck. She turned in his arms and gasped slightly as she took notice of the warm, soft glow that the room now took on.

"Everything looks amazing. Yes…I'm ready."

He led her over to the table, pulling the seat out for her. "I'll be right back." A few moments later he joined her at the table, setting a plate down in front of her. Before taking his seat he placed a soft kiss at her temple before taking his seat.

Kenneth briefly blessed the food before digging in.

"Bon appetite."

Simone was impressed with his cooking skills. She closed her eyes as she took a bite of the jumbo shrimp. Kenneth set mesmerized as he watched as she licked the sauce from her lips. She opened her eyes and found him staring. Taking a sip of wine she smirked at him. He couldn't help but return her smile. The two engaged in easy conversation as they enjoyed the excellent meal he'd prepared. After clearing their plates, he asked if she wanted to dance. The smooth sounds of Luther Vandross and various other R&B legends helped to set the mood. Then to her surprise, he began singing softly in her ear along with the music. Lifting her head off of his shoulder she stopped dancing momentarily, looking him in the eyes. "You have an amazing voice!" she exclaimed.

He chuckled slightly. "Thank you." Placing a soft kiss on her ear, he began dancing again. As they continued dancing, Kenneth unconsciously stroked her hair as he swayed with her, sending tingles down her spine.

A soft moan escaped her lips before she could stop it, silently hoping he hadn't heard. Just then his arms tightened around her waist, pulling her closer.

"Simone?"

She raised her head once again to look him in the eyes. In that moment no words were needed. Silently he took her hand as together they blew out the candles before heading upstairs.

———

Entering his bedroom, Kenneth looked over at Simone, noticing that she hadn't moved from where she now stood, just inside the doorway. Her expression on her face belying the nerves she felt. He pulled her close, wrapping his arms around her waist.

"Nervous?"

Simone simply nodded her head, "A little."

"We don't have to if you're not ready, if you don't want to."

She looked deep into his eyes, taking comfort in what she saw as Denise's words filtered into her mind: *He's a good man Simone. Take it one step at a time.*

"Why me?" Kenneth asked suddenly.

"Why you what?"

"After all this time, why me, why now?"

"There was a quiet innocence about you that masked your fire. A fire that burned with an alluring intensity, it was something unlike anything I've ever experienced. Like a moth to a flame you drew me in." Her words hit him and hit him hard. So it began.

Hearing her breathlessly concede to her desire was almost his undoing.

Placing his hands atop her shoulders, he slowly eased the straps down her arms. Sliding the soft material down the rest of her body, over her shapely hips and down her legs, revealing a cream-colored lace bra and matching thong.

Reaching her ankles, he eased each shoe off of her feet, before taking his lips on a slow journey back up her body. Simone shook with wanting and with the effort it took not to think about the scar; something which—for now, he was clearly oblivious to. Her knees buckled slightly as he placed feather soft kisses near her center.

Slowly rising to his feet, his hands glided up her thighs and over her hips, caressing and then cupping her backside. Lifting her effortlessly in his arms he headed towards the bed. Not wanting her to leave his arms, Kenneth lowered them both to the bed and covered her body with his, continuing to kiss her intimately. After a few moments, rising up, he quickly unbuttoned his shirt before pulling his undervest over his head. Caressing her full breast, he tweaked first one nipple and then the other as they strained against the lacy material. He quickly unfastened it.

"You're so beautiful."

Lowering his head, he began placing feather soft kisses along the column of her neck. Proceeding lower, he greedily covered her sensitive breast with his mouth. After paying due diligence to one, he eagerly attended to the other. Simone arched her body into his as the sensations flowed through her body. So long had it been since she allowed herself to, since she wanted to...*feel*, this way. Kenneth began his decent even lower, trailing kisses over her stomach until he reached the lacy thong covering her treasure. Sitting back on his heels, he swallowed hard.

"Are you sure?"

Simone simply nodded her head. She refused to think past this moment.

He stood in a trance as he began unfastening his pants before taking off his shoes. His eyes never left hers as he stood before her in only a pair of black boxer briefs. Simone's mouth watered at the bulge she saw outlined in them. His body was beautiful. Pulling back the linens, settling in he pulled her into his arms.

Running his hand up her thigh, he squeezed her soft, round derriere. She gasped as his hand found its way between her legs, stroking her now wet folds before slowly inserting a finger. Simone screamed out in pleasure.

After a few moments he withdrew his hand, removing her thong along with it. He kissed her deeply before once again making his way down her body, spreading her legs. She held her breath in anticipation, but Kenneth was in no hurry. He wanted to prolong this long awaited moment. He still had trouble believing he was here, with her, in this moment. He leisurely placed the softest of kisses along the inside of her thighs, massaging and caressing them in kind. Then, without notice, he kissed her, there. Parting her folds with his tongue, causing her to once again cry out as she gripped the sheets. Keeping a soft yet firm grip on her thighs, he didn't let up until she screamed her release. Reaching for the condom he'd placed on the nightstand, he quickly sheathed himself. Hovering over her entrance momentarily he said,

"Look at me," Her eyes fluttered before opening.

"I promise…I won't hurt you." He looked deep in her eyes as he spoke those words. She didn't respond, there was no need. Wrapping her arms around his neck, pulling him down, drowning herself in his kisses as he gradually filled her snug space.

In that instant, one word came to his mind: *Heaven.*
Kenneth paused briefly, closing his eyes amazed by the feel
of her, as he allowed her body to adjust. Then their dance
began. Settling into a slow, easy rhythm as if it was second
nature. She had begun grounding her hips into his and once
Simone felt comfortable enough to wrap her legs around his
waist, Kenneth let go and gave into his desire.

His hands and mouth roamed her body. Joining his
hands with hers, he looked deep into her eyes, placing her
arms above her head. Simone held his stare as an intense
feeling began to build, starting at her core. Closing her eyes
she held onto him as the intensity of her orgasm rocked her
body, his name echoing as she screamed her release. Several
more thrusts, burying his face against her sweat-drenched
neck; Kenneth grunted and moaned his release.

Chapter 29

As the first rays of light danced across the room and onto her face, Simone slowly opened her eyes. Shifting ever so slightly, she jumped as she came against Kenneth's warm, hard body, not use to the feeling of having someone there. Laying eyes on his handsome face as he slept peacefully, she instantly relaxed. She watched him sleep for another minute before gently easing out of bed. She had always been an early riser and didn't want to disturb him. Thankful for the soft, plush carpet, she tiptoed quietly across the room and headed into the bathroom to take a shower.

Entering the large door-less shower, Simone stepped in letting the hot water flow over her body, closing her eyes; she allowed her mind to wonder back to last night. A part of her was over the moon—the way he made love to her, the way he made her feel. The way he caused her body to spiral out of control, over and over again, well into the wee hours of the morning—her thighs clenched, the soreness between them all too real. The other part of her was fearful. Had they moved too fast, was there substance to his promise. The biggest question that plagued her was, would she allow herself to trust him, to let him in completely, to—love him. Everything about him was genuine and passionate. He made her feel so special. And then a more sinister thought popped into her head, *was there someone else in his life?* They had briefly talked about significant others and he had said he wasn't seeing anyone. She wouldn't be naive enough to believe that she was the only woman who had been left feeling this way after being in his presence. After feeling those skilled hands, that skilled tongue, those soft lips—

"I hope you saved some hot water for me," he uttered these words against her ear. He had managed to walk in without her noticing, taking advantage of the door-less entry. Momentarily caught off guard by the intrusion, her body reacted instantly to him. Grabbing the loofah off of the built in shelf, lathering it up, he proceeded to wash and sculpt her body. A shiver was her body's response to his ministrations. He grinned knowingly against her neck as he helped rinse the suds from her body. Turning to face him, she couldn't help but return his smile.

"Shall I return the favor?" she asked playfully, taking hold of his engorged member.

He closed his eyes briefly as he enjoyed the feel of her touch. Opening his eyes, now darkened with desire, easing himself away, he grabbed the condom he'd placed on the shelf. Quickly protecting them, he hosted her up in his arms.

"Later."

Placing her back against the cool marble, she gasped as he once again entered her body. He moved in and out with such an intensity that quickly had her building once again. She began to pant and moan loudly as the familiar feeling build within her. Feeling her feminine walls clench around him was his undoing, as this time they reached their climax together.

Chapter 30

Later that morning, after their steamy shower, Simone now sat watching a half-naked Kenneth prepare breakfast. Holding the mug he'd just given her—accompanied by a quick kiss on the lips—she watched as he moved around the kitchen, gathering ingredients for French toast and omelets. A warm, comforting feeling washed over her as she watched him prepare their meal. Several minutes later, he placed her plate in front of her as he took his seat beside her at the breakfast bar. They were silent a long while as they eagerly replenished the calories they'd burned off, both last night and this morning. Kenneth who had finished first, sat back in his chair silently watching Simone; he still could not believe she was here, eating breakfast, wearing only his t-shirt.

Placing her fork down, Simone looked up and found him staring.

"Can I help you Mr. Daniels?" she raised an eyebrow as she smirked at him.

He returned her smile as he leaned over and placed a kiss on her neck.

"Nope, I'm just happy that you're here."

"Me too," she responded honestly.

"Do you have anything planned for this weekend?"

"No nothing planned, surprisingly. I usually try and give myself at least one weekend free from work. Why?"

Kenneth chuckled.

"I was just wondering when's the last time you've actually been out to see a movie."

Simone seriously had to ponder this question. "You know? I really cannot remember."

"Well how bout it?"

She looked down at her appearance before raising her eyes to meet his. He laughed.

"Of course I can take you home to grab a change of clothes."

She arched her eyebrow at him as she smiled, "Oh really? Am I coming back here?"

"Are you not?" he fired back. They stared each other down before cracking up.

"I don't mind."

Kenneth was thrilled. "Okay great," he hesitated before asking his next question. "Tomorrow my mother is having Sunday dinner at her home. I know it is last minute but I would love it if you would join me."

Simone was both flattered and caught off guard, his question taking her by surprise.

"You want me to meet your family? Your mother?" She asked.

"Yes, I do. I've already spoken to them about you."

"You have?" her eyes wide. This really surprised her.

"Yes. I've talked to my mother about you, more so in a professional capacity. She has this annoying habit however, of being able to read me better than I know."

"Meaning?" she asked grinning.

"She has probably had an idea for some time now about how I've felt about you."

Simone blushed, flattered by his honesty and revelation.

"So, what do you say?" She was quiet for a few moments as she thought on everything he had said.

"Okay…I'll go with you."

His smile was wide and instant as he stood and embraced her. Lifting her up out of her chair, he placed wet kisses all over her face and neck. Simone squealed with laughter. Sitting her down on top of the counter he moved between her legs, placing his hands on her hips. Simone casually rested her arms on his shoulders as her right hand lightly caressed his soft-cropped hair. She closed her eyes as he continued to place soft kisses along her chin and down her neck. As the subtle contact was starting to affect her, he pulled back suddenly. Opening her eyes she found him staring at her, smiling.

"You're so bad," she said. He laughed slightly as he helped her down. "Come on woman." He took her hand as they headed upstairs. Twenty minutes later they were in his car heading to her place.

On the way over, their conversation was causal and the other moments of silence were filled by the random selection of songs from his iPod. A short time later they entered her apartment. Simone was laughing at something funny he had said as they walked into the main foyer. It was around 1:00 pm and Charles and Gladys were in the kitchen having lunch. She greeted them casually as they walked over to where they sat. Both of them smiled.

"Morning Gladys, Charles. I'd like you to meet Kenneth Daniels. Kenny, meet Charles and Gladys." Charles smiled as he stood holding his hand out.

"It is great to see you again," a genuine smile on his face. Kenneth smiled as he returned the handshake. Turning to Gladys Kenneth held out his hand to shake hers, but she immediately pulled him into a light embrace.

"Good to meet you."

"Likewise, it's a pleasure." Turning to Simone Gladys asked if she wanted something to eat. "There is plenty left over if you two would like to join us." Her and Charles had just sat down to eat the club sandwiches and veggie chips she'd prepared.

Simone looked at Kenneth, "Would you like to?"

Kenneth couldn't have been happier. The invitation wasn't anything major, but the fact that she was willingly inviting him was a big deal.

"Sure I'd love to, thank you."

"Okay great. Yes, Gladys we'd be glad to. I'll be back in a few minutes." she replied suddenly remembering what she had on, "I need to change."

Kenneth had given her a simple white t-shirt and a pair of grey sweats to throw on. As she headed towards her bedroom, a warm, fuzzy feeling came over her as she had glanced to the scene. While Gladys quickly put together two sandwiches for her and Kenneth, he'd taken a seat beside Charles and they quickly started up a discussion about the latest in sports news from the weekend paper.

After an amazing lunch, where the conversation had been plentiful and the laughs endless, they had decided to forgo going to the movie theater. Deciding instead to pop some popcorn and watch something in Simone's at home theatre. Kenneth decided to stay over since they were already there. As they once again cuddled together in her king sized bed, the last thought in her mind before giving into her exhaustion was, *this weekend couldn't have been more perfect.*

Chapter 31

Pulling up to the huge wrought iron gate Kenneth wound down his window to punch in the access code. Simone who had been quiet for the majority of the drive sat anxiously in the passenger seat. Kenneth took her hand in his as he waited for the gates to open. She looked over at him, her constant peace, and smiled.

Beautiful foliage lined the pebbled driveway leading up to the house. Entering the circular driveway Simone gasped; the house was huge.

"Wow this is amazing! So beautiful."

"I love it here. They built it from the ground up." Kenneth responded as he came to a stop and got out. Just as he was helping her out of the car, his mother opened up the main door. Taking Simone's hand, they walked towards the house. There was a huge smile on her face as she walked out with the twins-- his niece Michelle and nephew Michael in tow.

"Uncle Kenny!" the twins screamed as they rushed him. He laughed as they jumped in his arms. After placing them back down, he walked over and hugged his mother.

"Hey mama."

"Hello son!" Jackie said as she embraced her youngest.

"Oh! Who is that pretty lady?" Michelle asked noticing Simone first. Taking her hand in his again he introduced her, "This is my friend Simone. Can you guys say hello?"

"You mean your girlfriend? That's what mama said!" Michelle blurted out; she was her mother's child. Simone's face grew warm with embarrassment, feeling slightly out of her element.

"Michelle," Jackie warned, even as the slightest of smiles appeared on her face.

Kenneth had to hold back his laughter.

"Hello Miss Simone," they said simultaneously.

"Hello Michelle. Hello Michael." Simone leaned down and held out her hand. To her surprise, both kids threw their tiny arms around her. Her heart melted instantly.

Kenneth's heart swelled. As they released her Kenneth turned to introduce his mother.

"Simone, this is my mother Jackie Daniels. Mom, this is Simone Caines."

"It's a pleasure to meet you Ms. Daniels." Simone said as she held out her hand.

Jackie smiled, "I hardly think that it's fair that my grand babies get hugs and I'm expected to settle for a handshake." she teased pulling her into a warm embrace.

"And please honey, call me Jackie." she said releasing her.

Simone smiled, "Okay."

Kenneth looked on at the moment and couldn't have been happier.

"Okay guys let's head inside." Jackie said taking hold of the twins' hands. Kenneth walked up to Simone, placing his arm around her shoulders as they followed inside.

If Simone had been impressed with the outside appearance, she was blown away by the interior.

"Your mom designed all of this?" she asked

"Yes she did." Kenneth stated with pride.

As they walked down the hallway towards the kitchen, he could hear Kendra talking. "Brace yourself," he whispered in her ear as they rounded the corner. Simone chuckled. Entering the living room he walked over to where Kendra and Thomas stood talking with James. "Hey big head!" he said enveloping her in a bear hug.

"Boy put me down!" Kendra shouted as she laughed. He placed a wet kiss on her cheek before putting her down. "What's up Thomas? This one still giving you a hard time?" he joked as he shared a brotherly hug with his brother in law.

"What can I say?" was Thomas' non-committal answer.

"James, how are you?" Kenneth asked after sharing a heartfelt hug with him.

"Hanging in there. It's good to see you Ken," James returning his embrace.

"Kendra, Thomas, James, I'd like you to meet Simone Caines. Simone, this is my sister Kendra and her husband Thomas."

"Pleased to meet you Simone," like her mother, she instantly embraced her. "My brother hasn't stopped talking about you." Kendra teased, ignoring the glare on her brother's face.

"Honey cut it out." Thomas said as he too gave Simone a quick hug.

Surprisingly Simone was no longer feeling out of place, finding the playful banter entertaining.

"It's great to finally meet you all. And thank you for having me. Kenneth has told me such wonderful things about you."

"Thank you for saying that girl, but knowing this one," Kendra nodded her head in Kenneth's direction, "I can only imagine the one-sided stories he's told you."

Everyone laughed.

A short time later, after having blessed the food they all set around the dining room table. The laughs and great conversation were as hearty as the food on which they feasted.

"So is everything sorted for the banquet next week mama?" Kenneth asked after setting his fork down.

"I have no idea son, you would need to ask your sister. I've been effectively banned from any participation." Kenneth laughed as he shook his head.

"Why am I not surprised."

"Oh please brother. You know how mama is. She can't sit still for too long, hence the reason she still hasn't officially retired yet!" Kendra stated pointedly, her response eliciting a laugh from everyone.

"That's true. Do you think she is having second thoughts about leaving her company in your 'capable hands'?" he teased. Ignoring his question, Kendra turned to Simone.

"Simone will you be attending or has my brother neglected to invite you?" she asked playfully, ignoring the mean look Kenneth cut her.

"Cut it out you two. " Jackie admonished.

Simone couldn't help but smile as she responded. "He had asked me yes, but unfortunately I have to go away for business. I did mention that if I'm able to get everything tied up I would try and get back."

"Oh okay."

Changing the direction of the conversation she looked at Simone and asked,

"So Simone, how is my son making out?"

Kenneth choked on his water while Kendra busted out laughing. Simone just smiled, not surprised by the question.

"He is doing an amazing job. He is innovative, forward thinking and a great leader. I have been known to have high expectations and standards, but he has not had a problem meeting and superseding any of them." She looked at him and smiled. Everyone including Kenneth was momentarily left speechless—Kenneth especially. Her words had been about business, but the look in her eyes and the conviction with which she spoke them, said so much more.

Chapter 32

Standing in the main foyer, Simone and Kenneth said goodbye to his family.

"Simone it was wonderful meeting you. You're welcome here anytime okay? With or without my son." Jackie said as she again hugged her.

"Thank you Jackie, I'll remember that."

Turning she said good-bye to Kendra, Thomas and the twins, who again hugged her before running off to play.

"Simone call me anytime you need help with this one okay." Kendra joked as she hugged her.

"Honey," Thomas warned as he hugged Simone.

Walking over to hug her brother Kendra smiled, "Oh you know I'm only messing with you. Love you little brother," she said as she squeezed him tightly. "I really like her Ken," she whispered in his ear before pulling away.

"Love you too sis. Thomas, see you later bro."

Lastly he walked over to where his mother stood with James. Giving James a heartfelt hug before he turned to embrace his mother.

"Thanks for dinner mama, it was great."

"You're welcome son, I'm so glad you were able to come. She's an amazing woman. I like her."

"Thank you mama." Kenneth's heart swelled. Taking Simone's hand they waved one final goodbye before heading out to his car.

As they pulled off, both were quiet, reliving the night's events. Kenneth was over the moon, not sure how the night was to play out, but thrilled that it had gone better than he expected. Simone couldn't remember the last time she had felt so happy. His family was wonderful and had welcomed her and made her feel at home. This weekend had definitely been a game changer for them both, big time.

—

The next couple of weeks had flown by in a haze. The day before the banquet Simone had informed Kenneth that she wouldn't be able to attend. The meetings were running longer than she had expected. He had said he'd understood but she had heard the disappointment in his voice. The day of, Simone had been informed that they should be able to finish up things by early afternoon. She immediately phoned

Charles so that she could fly back to surprise Kenneth at the banquet.

"Charles I need you to call Frank and arrange to have the jet pick me up. I should have everything squared off in the next hour or so. I need to leave New York by 6:00pm at the latest," she said, bypassing formalities and getting straight to the point as usual.

"Yes ma'am. Anything else?"

"Yes, have Gladys send my gown with you so that I can change on the flight back."

"Yes ma'am"

Three hours later she sat in the back of the Audi S8, finally on her way to the banquet. It had started at 7:30pm; glancing at her watch she saw that she would only be missing about forty-five minutes.

Kendra had done a bang up job and everything looked amazing. Kenneth did his best to shake his somber mood, wishing Simone could have been there. Not wanting to draw any attention away from his mother and her special night, he shook it off and tuned in to the next speaker. Several employees, friends and colleagues shared their stories, experiences and lessons learned under his mother's leadership. They were sad to see her go, but everyone still expressed their confidence in Kendra and her abilities to do her mother proud.

As the servers began bringing out the food, Kenneth excused himself to use the restroom. When he came out, he pulled his phone out to see if he'd had any messages from Simone. There were none, nor any missed calls.

That's strange, he thought. Her last meeting should've ended by now. He began to dial her number.

"I hope that's my number you're dialing." Simone said from behind him.

He spun around. "Simone? He rushed to her, hugging her to him tightly. "How did you? When did you?"

His reaction was everything. She couldn't stop smiling.

"I managed to tie up the loose ends early and called Charles and had him arrange for the jet to pick me up. I tried to get here earlier, I'm sorry."

"You have nothing to be sorry for, I'm just happy that you're here at all," he said before searing her with a kiss. "You look amazing! Thank you for coming."

"You're just in time anyway; they've only just started to serve the food. Come on. Everyone will be so excited that you're here."

Walking up to the table Kenneth announced, "Look who I found?"

"Simone! Oh baby I'm so glad you could make it!" Jackie gushed, as she stood and embraced her. Kendra and Thomas followed before everyone took their seats.

They had a blast the rest of the night. A local house band played an awesome variety of music throughout the evening and the food was amazing. Simone soon lost any trace of regret at not being there from the beginning. Kenneth also informed her that the whole event had been taped.

The nightmares and flashbacks had all but stopped since she and Kenneth had gotten together. His presence and overall positive outlook on things had had such a tremendous effect on her. What she felt for him she still couldn't put into words. They had made it official the day after his mother's banquet.

Kenneth's patience and understanding never wavered. If it was meant to last forever it would. He promised to do his part to restore the trust that had been broken. She in turn promised to do her best to meet him half way. In the not too distant future they would both do well to remember said promises.

Chapter 33

Walking into the kitchen after she had finished getting ready for work, Simone couldn't remember a time when she had felt so content and happy. As if to reconfirm her thoughts, her phone signaled she had a message. She smiled looking at the screen. It was from Kenneth. As she placed it on the counter, she noticed that Gladys had left a small stack of mail on the kitchen counter. She began thumbing through the stack when she suddenly gasped. It was if a bolt of lightning had struck her as the envelopes fell to the floor.

"No no no...!"

Simone began trembling uncontrollably. Tears she had held back for years began streaming down her face. She had told Dr. Phillips that she had felt something troubling was lingering but she just couldn't remember what. She had been told after sentencing that this day might come. So hard had she fought and toiled to forget him and her past that she had all but forgotten that this day would come.

"Jonesville Correctional Facility Parole Board."

Just then Gladys and Charles walked into the kitchen, both immediately noticing her distressed state. Turning away abruptly as she did not need them to fret over her, she grabbed her iPhone and briefcase and headed back towards her room.

"Charles I'm not going into work today."

      Without a backwards glance she continued down the hall. Entering her bedroom, throwing her briefcase onto the bed, she hesitated before contacting Denise to let her know she wasn't coming in and to cancel any meetings. She didn't want to risk calling for she knew Denise would pick up on it immediately. She sent her a text instead. After she'd sent it, she immediately turned her phone off, stripped out of her clothes and climbed back under the covers. As she reached out and touched the button which lowered the blackout shades, one tear fell...and then another and another. Pulling her knees to her chest Simone continued to sob, feeling completely numb, the pain of the past already consuming her. She stayed this way for forever it seemed until she had drifted off to sleep; suddenly feeling exhausted from how drained she felt.

—

Kenneth walked into work looking forward to seeing Simone after the amazing weekend they'd had. He had a blast at his mother's party and to his delight everyone loved Simone and the feelings seemed to be mutual. Reaching his office, he placed down his things as he reached for the phone on his desk. There was no answer at her desk. He thought to call Denise but decided to pop by after he grabbed his morning cup of coffee. Five minutes later, crossing the carpeted section of the separate waiting area outside Simone's office, he walked up to Denise's opened door and knocked. Her back was facing the open doorway. She had arrived only a few minutes earlier, her briefcase and other items still sitting atop her desk. She hadn't moved since receiving the text message.

"Good Morning!" his cheery voice momentarily broke through the confusion clouding Denise's mind as she re-read the text she'd received:

Not coming in. Cancel my meetings.

The bluntness isn't what bothered her, nor was the fact that it was via text—which she had found to be odd, it was the vagueness of her message that had immediately puzzled her. She was just about to call Simone as soon as she had read it but that was when Kenneth had walked in. Placing the phone on her desk, she fixed her face to mirror his mood before turning around.

"Someone is in a good mood this morning! Good morning to you too."

"How was your weekend?"

"My weekend was pretty good, a relaxed one. And yourself? Did you guys have a good time at the banquet?"

Kenneth tried and failed—not that he minded, to curb the huge grin that appeared on his face. "Yes we did. It was touching to see how important my mom was to so many people. She will definitely be missed. The party went on until the wee hours." They shared a laugh before he continued, "I came to see if you ladies wanted anything from the 10th floor. I was going to pop down to get a pastry or something to go with my coffee."

"I'm okay for now thanks; I'm just getting in myself. Once I get settled I'll get myself sorted," she hesitated just then, assuming he didn't know that Simone wasn't here. A fact that she had found strange as well—Simone usually beat her in to work.

Kenneth took note of not only her hesitancy but also the fact that Simone's office was still in darkness. He tried to come up with a casual way of inquiring about her whereabouts without appearing to be fishing for information. He decided against it and would just wait to hear from her; the moment quickly becoming awkward.

"Okay I'll let you get settled. Have a good day," he had started to turn when Denise spoke.

"I'll let her know that her tardiness caused her to miss out on your generosity this morning," she joked in an attempt to diffuse the awkwardness. It worked. Kenneth chuckled slightly as he spoke, "Okay. I'll talk to you later."

As soon as she heard his footsteps step off of the carpeted area onto the tile leading back down the hallway, she snatched up her cellphone and dialed Simone's number. The call immediately went to voicemail. She hung up and called again, and again. *What is going on??* She tried calling her at home, dialing both her house and home office phone—no answer. *This isn't making any sense.* She thought as she began pacing her office. She was tempted to hop in her car and head straight over to Simone's apartment. She couldn't though, not at the moment anyway. There were several meetings that she had to reschedule, important meetings—glancing at her watch—one that was scheduled to start in the next forty-five minutes. Sitting behind her desk she picked up her phone to respond to Simone's text:

Your ass better call me back ASAP.

She cursed inwardly before taking a deep breath to collect herself, before getting started on her now tedious task of rescheduling. Picking up the phone she paused before dialing Kenneth's extension, his voicemail picked up. Figuring he was still downstairs, she left him a message. She felt it was the least she could do.

When Kenneth returned back to his office, he noticed the message indicator was flashing on his phone. He quickly rounded his desk to retrieve his messages, hoping there was one from Simone; he was mistaken. It was Denise informing him that she had called out sick.

Chapter 34

Kenneth found it difficult but he did his best to wait a couple of hours before reaching out to Simone. She seemed fine when they had spoken last night so he forced himself not to worry; figuring a last minute business call or meeting elsewhere was her reason for being out and not replying to his message. Looking at the time, he saw that the rest of the morning went by rather quickly. Having been so caught up with his latest project, Kenneth hadn't had a chance to reach out to Simone yet. Retrieving his iPhone from his briefcase, he was both disappointed and a little concerned that there were no missed calls or messages from her. Taking note of the time and no longer able to focus, he grabbed his wallet, keys and cellphone and headed out to grab something for lunch and get some fresh air.

Stepping out of the building, as he walked the two short blocks to the deli he tried calling her cell; it went straight to voicemail.

That's odd. He tried once more—voicemail again. As he continued walking, he passed a new Thai restaurant that had finally opened. Deciding to try something from there instead, he entered the establishment. Forcing himself again not to worry Kenneth busied himself with trying to decide what to eat. Noticing there was a long line; while he waited he called Denise to see if she wanted anything.

"Hello?"

"Hey Denise, that new Thai place you had mentioned has finally opened. I'm here now and figured I'd be nice and see if you wanted to try anything."

She laughed before responding, "How thoughtful! Actually yes I wouldn't mind trying something," she paused glancing at her watch, "You left for lunch early? I would've walked with you."

"Yeah, I had been going nonstop since arriving at work trying to keep busy and needed some air." Denise immediately caught the underlining message behind what he said; she hadn't heard anything more from Simone either, aside from her text this morning--*which is odd,* she thought.

"Oh alright, well I've actually just finished off what I needed to do for the morning so I can meet you there.

"Cool, there's a bit of a line anyway so you should get here just in enough time to look at the menu before ordering.

"Ok, I'll see you in a few."

Five minutes later Denise entered the restaurant, walking over to where Kenneth stood. Her timing was perfect as there were still two people in front of him.

After placing their orders, they stepped off to the side and waited. Kenneth no longer able to keep his thoughts to himself, he turned to Denise.

"Have you heard from Simone? I thought it was odd this morning that she wasn't at work yet and she hasn't responded to any of my messages. And now her phone is off and going straight to voicemail." The worried expression now on her face only heightened his.

"She had messaged me this morning to tell me she wasn't coming in. I tried calling her myself and got the same thing. I found it strange that she messaged instead of calling. I've had to cancel and reschedule all of her meetings for today."

"Order number 39!"

"That's us," Kenneth paid for and collected their food before they headed back to the office.

"Thank you for lunch. Next time it's my treat." Denise said once they arrived back.

"You're welcome and I'll hold you to that. I'll let you know if I hear from her."

"So will I."

With that they went their separate ways.

—

Five o'clock rolled around and Kenneth still hadn't heard from Simone. Grabbing his things he headed out, his mind made up. He was going to stop by.

Thirty minutes later, using his swipe key he entered the garage. Pulling into the guest parking space, a small sense of relief washed over him seeing all of her cars in their designated spots. Getting out of the car, he walked quickly to the elevator.

Reaching her floor, when the doors opened Charles stood there waiting for him. He can't say he was surprised. During one of the times he'd been here Charles had shown him the extensive security and surveillance system that he'd installed himself. He had also learned that Charles wasn't just Simone's driver but her bodyguard as well.

Charles held his hand out in greeting as Kenneth stepped off the elevator.

"Mr. Daniels, It's good to see you."

"Charles, likewise," a slight pause and then, "Is she here?"

For the first time since meeting him, Kenneth noticed a look of what? Unease, sadness was present on his face.

"Yes she's here but…" Before he could continue, Kenneth made a beeline for her suite.

Charles grabbed a hold of his arm. "Ken wait…" Turning back to face him, to Kenneth it was clear he was struggling with his words. Something was clearly wrong.

"She's…had a rough day okay?"

His heart sank. *What the hell does that mean?* Charles let him go and he slowly walked to her room. Opening the door slowly, he was puzzled as to why her room was in complete darkness.

"Simone?" he called out to her but received no answer. Using the light from his phone he illuminated a path over to her bed. Turning on the lamp on the nightstand, he found her fast asleep. As he breathed a sigh of relief, concern still filled his mind.

Why is she still asleep? Taking off his suit jacket he gently sat down beside her, watching her for a long while. His mind was full of unanswered questions. Sighing, he stood and headed into the bathroom, hoping a hot shower would clear his head.

Twenty minutes later, having changed his clothes, he climbed into bed and embraced her. Simone shifted slightly without waking. He nuzzled her neck and breathed in deeply as he caressed her body. Still in a deep sleep she moaned lightly as she turned over and snuggled closer, placing feather soft kisses on his chest.

He placed his lips to her ear as he whispered, "Simone baby, wake up."

Her eyes fluttered before slowly opening, she gasped

"What are you doing here?" even as she asked this, she was immediately comforted by his presence.

"You had to know I would be worried about you. What's going on Simone? I know something is wrong," he queried, tilting her chin so that she could look at him.

"Talk to me," he pleaded.

"I don't want to talk about it right now."

"Simone…" She silenced him as she kissed him passionately. She had missed him terribly and her hunger for him overshadowed the pain.

"Please…just make love to me," she moaned breathlessly. Kenneth's body immediately responded, he knew he wouldn't get any answers if he pressed her. He let it go for now, giving into the affects of her kisses. She wore one of his t-shirts; pulling it over her head before stripping out of his boxer briefs, he covered her body with his. Hovering over for a moment before plunging deep, Simone cried out as she pulled him down to her. Rolling over, Simone straddled his waist, placing her hands on his chest. She rode him with such a passion it was almost his undoing. Wanting to feel every part of him, rising up again, she slowly sank back down, clenching her muscles settling into a slow, deep rhythm. Placing her beneath him again, he moved within her with such urgency, Simone's body began to spiral at the onset of her orgasm. Soon she cried out with such intensity as her climax shook her to the core. Soon after Kenneth moaned loudly, collapsing on to her body.

Chapter 35

Hours later Simone lay awake as sleep eluded her. Glancing over, her smile was bittersweet as she lightly ran her hand down his handsome face. The smile quickly faded as sadness crept into her heart. Quietly she eased out of bed, grabbing her black silk robe. Securing the tie around her waist, she headed out of her room. Entering the kitchen she spotted the envelope on the counter. She grabbed it and an unfinished bottle of wine. Pouring herself a glass, her heart and mind heavy, she headed towards the great room. Walking into her spacious living room she sat down on the huge sofa in front of the floor to ceiling windows, placing the envelope next to her. Lost in thought she gazed out over the breathtaking view, its beauty lost on her.

Her calm demeanor contrasted with the war of thoughts plaguing her at this hour in the morning. Kenneth had been so open, patient and understanding. He gave her every reason to trust him and in turn to do the same, and yet here she was. Withdrawing within herself, falling back into the old habit of dealing with it on her own. But Simone knew why. She had opened up to an extent, but there was still so much he didn't know. Not having given into or even acknowledged any sort of fear since...Simone was afraid that once Kenneth found out, he would leave. How could he understand or not see her as something other than the powerhouse she had worked so hard to become. Sighing, Simone pressed two fingers to her forehead attempting to ward off the impending headache. Tonight was so beautiful; their lovemaking was...Simone instantly smiled at the thought. Just the thought of how he had made her feel...

"I wondered where you had disappeared to." Kenneth said
Simone gasped; she hadn't heard him come down the stairs.

He came and set next to her, concern etched on his face as he took her hand in his.
"Look at me Simone."
After what seemed an eternity, she turned and looked at him, a single tear slid down her cheek.
"Can you please talk to me? Whatever it is, do you really think after all this time and after everything that has grown and strengthened between us, that I will just walk away? You know what kind of man I am, trust me."

"I do trust you. The moments we've shared, that I've only had with you. That glimmer of hope breaks through the darkness. I feel like I can be myself. You see me for who I am. It still scares me though."

"Why.."

She stared blankly back at him, unable to bring myself to utter the words past the chokehold of fear that grips her at the thought. But Simone knew why, it's the reason why she threw herself into becoming what she is now.

"You will never be anything because of what I've taken from you!"

The echoing of those words causes Simone to withdraw.

"I..I.."

His eyes pleaded with her, "I *can't. I just...can't* ".

"I'm sorry."

Taking her hands in his he moved closer, proceeding with such caution, as if dealing with a timid child and not the strong, independent powerhouse of a woman.

In that moment, there was nothing left to be said. It was the quiet confidence that he possessed that had broken through and made what she had deemed impossible. It had breathed light into a dark place, turning it into a definite possibility. Simone had deemed this a lost cause for so many years. She sighed heavily as another tear slid down her cheek, whilst gazing back into dark brown orbs that reflected with confirmation, every feeling she felt. Picking up the envelope, she handed it to him.

Taking it out of her hand he looked down at the envelope reading the front. Looking back up at her, he had no idea what this meant.

"I don't understand," he looked at her confused.

She took a deep breath before revealing and reliving a story she hadn't had to share in over a decade.

"When I was thirteen I lost both of my parents in a car accident. They had gone to a party and on the way home a drunk driver ran a red light, killing them both instantly. In one night my whole life changed. The only other family I had was my maternal grandmother. I hadn't seen her physically in almost 7 years. We had been close before but she had remarried and moved to the states. Her husband had passed away the year before my parents were killed. When she was notified about what had happened she immediately flew back home, took me in and became my legal guardian and my everything."

Kenneth felt for her, knowing what it had felt like to lose his father. He couldn't imagine losing his mother as well. He still had no idea what this had to do with the letter he still held, wondering if it had to do with the man who killed her parents. He asked her.

"No, I had found out about 5 years ago that he had died of liver cancer in prison. That was his third strike; he was never getting out of jail regardless."

"Oh okay." Simone had become quiet again; he wondered what else there could be.

"During my first year in college I met a guy named Stephen Johnson. He was a junior and a business major as well, so we shared many of the same classes. He was one of the more popular guys on campus. At that time I had a close circle of friends but still kept to myself, but he was someone who everyone knew. He was outgoing and had this unassuming way about him that people automatically gravitated to. He became one of my best friends and after a year of friendship, he asked me to be his girlfriend. Things started out great in the beginning, but soon he became more and more possessive and controlling. I loved him and had seen a future with him, but it became too much. The last straw was during an argument he gripped my arms so tightly he left bruises. After that I wanted out before things got worse. At first he seemed to be coming to terms with it, but I later found out it was only because he thought I only needed time to calm down. Once he realized I wasn't going to take him back he became more aggressive. I eventually had to get a restraining order.

He had graduated soon after that and from what I was told had moved back home. A few months later however, he had come back into town for homecoming, as a lot of his friends were still there. On the last night of homecoming I had seen friends of his at a party. They told me he'd been asking about me and that he'd changed but I wasn't interested. After talking with them, I left and went elsewhere before he showed up. I don't know how he found out where I lived because I stayed on campus while with him. I hadn't moved into the apartment that I shared with Denise until our final year.

Denise's boyfriend at the time had dropped me off. She was going to stay at his apartment. He owned a two-door car so his friend had to get out to let me out. I knew him but he was only a friend. Before walking off, I gave him a hug before heading to my place. I had just reached my door and unlocked it when Stephen rushed me, covering my mouth so I couldn't scream as he carried me inside. He stunk of liquor. He let me go, but said if I screamed he would kill me. He said he only wanted to talk, saying he wanted me back, he'd changed, etc. I told him I had moved on and to get out or I was calling the police." She paused as the tears that had filled her eyes now spilled down her cheeks. Kenneth moved to console her but she stayed him with her hand.

"Next thing I know he produced a knife…I tried to run and that's when he stabbed me in the back. I fell to the floor and then he…he raped me, then he stabbed me again in the stomach." Kenneth couldn't believe what he was hearing. His heart ached for her even as he became filled with rage.

"I laid there bleeding on the floor as he stood over me. Before leaving he said,

"You will never be anything because of what I've taken from you." And then he left. He left me there to die." Simone closed her eyes against the memory.

"Those words and the cold look in his eyes have haunted me ever since."

"How did you survive?"

"As I was about to lose consciousness, Denise had come in. She had forgotten something in her room. Her screams were the last thing I'd heard. I woke up in the hospital two weeks later. If she had been even a few minutes late or not come at all I would be dead."

"What happened to him?"

"He was charged with rape, assault with a deadly weapon and attempted manslaughter. He was sentenced to 25 years to life."

Kenneth sat there stunned in silence. He couldn't believe what he'd just heard. "When did you get it?" he asked, gesturing towards the letter.

"This morning. I was checking my mail before heading into work. When I saw it, I freaked out. I had forced myself to forget about the situation, let alone him possibly being paroled. It caught me so off guard I didn't know what to do."

He made another attempt to console her and this time she let him.

"Simone I'm sorry that happened to you. I'm sorry that you are hurting," he paused, lifting her chin so she would look at him, "I'm not going anywhere okay. I will stand by you through this and I do not see you as anything less. If anything, now in my eyes, I see you as an even stronger and braver woman." Standing, he held out his hand. "Come, let's go back to bed." She took his hand as they walked silently back to her room.

Chapter 36

Climbing under the covers, Kenneth pulled her into his arms and held her securely. She shed a few more tears before falling asleep. Kenneth however, could not sleep. He laid awake for a long while after, deep in thought. He had seen the scars but the fact that she had never brought attention to them, he was never curious enough to ask about them. He had figured that they were from some childhood accident.

Never in a million years would he have thought something so horrific was the story behind them. That she had finally decided to share all that she had with him, moved him deeply. Allowing herself to be so open, bearing her soul to him and being so vulnerable further cemented his feelings.

He was slowly but surely falling for her. Gazing upon her as she slept, lowering his head he kissed her cheek. He knew that he still had a long way to go in winning her heart. Soon he too drifted off to sleep.

—

The next morning, after showering together, Kenneth and Simone sat in the kitchen as Gladys prepared breakfast. After she'd awakened, belatedly Simone realized that she had forgotten to turn on her phone. She knew Denise had to have been worried out of her mind and was probably on the verge of inflicting bodily harm. As soon as she turned it on her phone lit up with notifications. She had 15 voicemails alone, all of which she figured were from Denise. Bypassing them she simply dialed her number. Denise picked up on the first ring.

"Yeah I wouldn't have listened to any of my messages either," she said in replace of hello. Her greeting caused Simone to smile instantly.

"I'm sorry Denise. I slept all day and just only realized I had left my phone turned off."

"Are you okay? You had me worried sick! What happened?"

"It's too much to talk about over the phone. Would you mind coming by?"

"Girl you know me better than that. I'm already on my way." Simone laughed out loud. "Okay then." hanging up she placed the phone down just as Kenneth reentered the room.

"Is she coming?" Kenneth asked once he'd retaken his seat.

"She was already on her way," she informed him. He chuckled slightly, "That's a great friend you have there."

—

When Denise arrived Kenneth went to watch a few games with Charles, to give them privacy. Simone told Denise everything that had happened and how Kenneth had showed up.

"I had figured he would. I'm glad one of us came by."

"I'm surprised you didn't."

"I decided to give you at least 24 hours to call me before I showed up." The two of them laughed at that statement.

Simone went on to tell her how she finally told Kenneth what had happened and about her parents and grandmother. She expressed how he took it better than she had expected.

"How did you expect him to react?" Denise asked.

"I don't know. But who wouldn't look at someone different after all that I've told him. I don't even know why I'm wasting either of our time." Simone sighed resting her head in her hands. Denise looked at her sympathetically. She knew this was hard for her and it pained Denise to see her like this, again, after all this time.

"Simone, look at me." Simone slowly raised her head, her eyes once again full of tears as they met Denise's. Denise wiped the ones that fell away before continuing.

"You're not wasting his time Simone, or yours. It's obvious he cares deeply for you."

"How do you know that?"

"I'm not blind. He tried to hide it, but there was genuine concern on his face and in his eyes when he came looking for you yesterday morning. Then he came here and he is still here so what does that tell you? Look all I'm saying is give the man the benefit of the doubt okay? He's a good man," she paused, "and fine!"

Laughing, Simone said, "Listen to you Mrs. Married."

Smiling, she said, "I know, but I have eyes. Seriously Simone, are you falling for him?"

Blushing, Simone lowered her head as she softly said, "Yes."

Denise hugged her, "Well from what I can tell the feeling is mutual. As I suggested to you before, just continue taking it one day at a time. You'll know when it's the right time to tell him. You've already decided to be honest with him about your situation and that says a lot."

"Okay, I'll try. I am grateful for him being in my life," she paused.

Hugging her best friend again, Simone shed a few tears, "And I am so grateful to have you in my life.

"Me too," she paused, "as if you could get rid of me." Denise replied returning her embrace. The two continued to talk casually and hung out for a few more hours. Kenneth walked back into the living room just as Denise stood.

"Sorry am I interrupting anything?"

Grabbing her purse, she smiled. "Not at all, I was just leaving." Walking over to him Denise hugged him. "Take good care of her."

"I will, I promise." he said as he hugged her back.

Simone and Kenneth watched as Denise walked to the elevator. Once the doors closed Kenneth turned to face her and asked, "How are you holding up pretty lady?"

"I'll be okay," she said smiling, "thank you for still being here."

Wrapping his arms around her, he held her close as he reached up and caressed her face.

"I'll be here for as long as you allow me to be."

"Okay."

"Okay. Are you ready for bed?

His question was asked innocently enough, but his intense gaze caused a shiver to travel down her spine; leaving her speechless. All she could do was nod. Kenneth smiled as he took her hand in his as they headed to the bedroom.

Epilogue

A month later

The week leading up to the hearing, Simone fought vehemently to keep busy. She refused to let it affect her day-to-day life. The night before the hearing Kenneth and Simone sat at the dining room table enjoying the dinner he had prepared. Gladys had the night off and she and Charles were out on one of their dates. Simone had been quiet for the majority of the night for which he understood. She was thankful to have him there regardless—he had told her a few weeks ago that he would never leave her side and hadn't since.

Theirs was a companionable silence as they lay in bed. Kenneth had thought Simone had fallen asleep until she rose up on her elbow and looked at him. Caressing his face she just looked at him for a long while.

"Thank you."
No other words were needed as she slowly lowered her head.

———

The next morning

Sitting outside the courtroom, Simone sat on one of the wooden benches that lined the hallway. A myriad of thoughts ran through her mind. Then, like always, it was as if he could sense when she needed him--Kenneth, who had been sitting quietly beside her, took her hand in his giving it a gentle yet reassuring squeeze. She turned to him and smiled in spite of the fact that everything within her wanted her to break down. He had become her strength. Moments later a court official walked out of the courtroom,

"Miss Caines they're ready for you."

She closed her eyes as she took a deep breath, a single tear rolling down her cheek.

Kenneth leaned in and placed the lightest of kisses on her temple before wiping the tear away.

"Look at me."

Slowly she turned to face him.

"You can do this."

Once again she closed her eyes as he hugged her. Pulling back he looked at her,

"Ready?"

Taking another deep breath, she nodded her head. Together they stood and walked in.

Kenneth took his seat as Simone walked ahead.

"Your honor, the court would like to call Simone Caines to the stand.

Made in the USA
Columbia, SC
20 November 2024

46689012R00124